To: Alec

With best wishes,

This first edition of
"The Call of Distant Drums"
was autographed by the Author

The Call of Distant Drums

William Pisani

JoNa Books
Bedford, Indiana

ISBN: 1-932673474

First Printing: July 2005

Cover design by JoNa Books Publishing Co.

JoNa Books Publishing Company
1611 J Street, Bedford, Indiana 47421

Printed in the United States of America

For my mother, who first taught me to love God, and

For my father, who first taught me to love the American Indian.

We hold it a noble task to rescue from oblivion those who deserve to be eternally remembered.
- Pliny

In Memory of the Weckquasgeek

TABLE OF CONTENTS

Chapter 1

The Hunt

An eagle soars on outspread wings, searching the plains below. Clouds of dust appear in the distance as warriors on horseback encircle the buffalo.

***

Lone Wolf rode his horse up to the edge of the overlook. Dust from the hunt covered his weathered face. Out of sight of the others, he broke for rest. How soothing the sun felt on his aging bones.

The cry of a bird pierced the silence. As Lone Wolf looked up, his heart began to race. Circling overhead was a white-headed eagle. Perhaps it was an omen foreshadowing his own death, for it was not uncommon for an experienced hunter to be killed during a buffalo hunt.

But he was not ready to die this day. He had yet to relinquish the title he held for over thirty snows, Warrior Chief of the Blackfoot-Blood. His son, Swift Elk, Lone Wolf reminded himself, had waited long enough. Time and again Swift Elk had proven himself among all others of the tribe. No warrior, other than Lone Wolf, wore as many battle scars across his chest, including one from the long swords of the hated white man.

What made it so difficult, then, to turn over to his only son the coveted headdress of Warrior Chief? And why had he never confided in Swift Elk how he felt—that he was proud of him, and deemed him worthy to be his successor some day.

Lone Wolf looked up again. The eagle continued to circle. He grew more fearful.

"I must tell Swift Elk before the sun sets," Lone Wolf spoke aloud for only himself to hear. "I must tell my son without further delay, before some misfortune befalls me and my voice is silenced forever—as was my father's."

Suddenly Lone Wolf heard distant drums from out of the East, the same drums he had heard from time to time throughout his years among the Blackfoot, his adopted people. But there were no tribes to the East, not for more than three days ride by horse.

A light breeze began to blow, causing the eagle feathers draped along his upright spear to flutter. It was early autumn, and the buffalo herds had returned to the Northern Plains where the grass was still green. The rays of the sun glittered off the buffalo carcasses scattered over the plains below. The hunt was good. There would be meat in the mountain lodges of the Blackfoot during the long winter ahead.

It was the buffalo, most ancient and revered creature of the plains, that provided for all the needs of his people. Its dried meat sustained them throughout the bleak winter months. Its thick fur kept them and their children warm against the brutal winds that blew across the plains. And its resilient hide covered their tepees, which could be moved quickly in pursuit of the buffalo herds upon which the Blackfoot depended.

As Lone Wolf's eyes again searched the plains, Swift Elk galloped up to the overlook to greet him.

"Father, have you seen my two kills today?"

"Yes, Swift Elk, I have watched you closely." Lone Wolf glanced toward the buffalo carcasses lying in the distance. "Young Hawk has three."

Swift Elk, turning his eyes away, did not answer.

"As for myself," Lone Wolf finally broke the silence, "I have sought the Great Buffalo, my arrow nearly finding its mark before the wary creature turned and fled."

Swift Elk recalled the legend he had first heard as a child: the Great Buffalo, last of an ancient species, was the grandfather Spirit of all the buffalo that roamed the plains. Only on rare occasions could the huge animal be seen. And only the greatest of hunters could ever dare to challenge this swift and cunning creature.

"For thirty snows," Lone Wolf continued, "I have searched for the Great Buffalo, hunting him each of the few times I have seen him. Since the very first sighting, I had hoped to fell this phantom of the plains. Its spirit could then return, at last, to the Spirit Land where it would rejoin the others of its kind who have long since disappeared."

"I wish that I, too, may finally see it," Swift Elk said.

"My arrows have come close, very close," Lone Wolf lamented, "but have never found their mark. I fear that time now is too fleeting for me to ever bring down this most elusive of creatures."

"Then I shall fell the Great Buffalo for you," Swift Elk said. "My third kill will put Young Hawk in his place, and prove myself to all — and to you, Father."

Again, came the piercing cry of a bird, circling overhead. They both looked up, shading their eyes.

"Father, the white-headed eagle."

"Yes, Swift Elk, I saw him earlier, which brings to mind something I must tell you. By the next moon..."

Before Lone Wolf could finish his words, Swift Elk caught a glimpse of the Great Buffalo, its massive bulk rising over the crest of a hill on the far side of the plains. When in full view, it stood nearly twice as high as the other buffalo.

"There he is, Father, I have finally seen him!" Swift Elk shouted, causing his horse to rear up. "This huge beast shall be my third kill, the most prized among hunters."

Swift Elk kicked his horse, forcing it to leap off the overlook, down to the slope below. With dust rising behind them, they raced across the plains in chase of the humped-back animal that stood silhouetted on the crest of the distant hill.

As his son rode off, Lone Wolf watched anxiously. He called out to him, "Be careful! I must speak to you before the day has passed."

Swift Elk charged up the face of the barren hill. The Great Buffalo stubbornly held its ground until the very last, snorting defiantly, its tail raised upward.

The young hunter closed in quickly on the huge creature. They both disappeared over the far side of the hill hunted followed by hunter, then reappeared out of a billow of dust. Again they disappeared, and then reappeared, the Great Buffalo running and dodging, with Swift Elk charging closely behind. Swift Elk reached back to position his spear for the kill.

The fleeing beast turned sharply near the top of the hill with Swift Elk still in pursuit. Suddenly Swift Elk's horse tripped and broke to the ground. Rider and horse rolled over each other, once, then again, as they tumbled to the foot of the slope.

Lone Wolf galloped across the plains to where his son lay motionless on the ground. He dismounted before his horse could come to a halt and ran to Swift Elk. Kneeling down, he held his son's body in his arms. The sweet scent of prairie grass hung in the air, along with the smell of the surrounding carnage.

"Swift Elk, how badly are you hurt?"

"Father," he answered with labored breath, looking up into Lone Wolf's eyes, "I am sorry I...could not..."

Lone Wolf grabbed a small buckskin pouch tied to his waist, then touched it to Swift Elk's heart. Turning toward the sun in the western sky, he prayed aloud:

4

"Take me, Great Spirit. Take me in his place."

Other hunters of the tribe, seeing Lone Wolf holding his son, galloped over and dismounted. They gathered silently around the two. A latecomer, unaware of what was happening, rode into the group, shouting about his recent kill and pointing for all to see.

"Be quiet, you fool," one of the older warriors scolded him.

As Swift Elk looked up at his father, his eyes began to close.

"No, Swift Elk, you cannot die! I must speak to you before your Spirit leaves this world. You have proven yourself worthy. You are to succeed me as Warrior Chief of our people."

Swift Elk's eyes closed.

"Have you heard my words, Swift Elk?" Lone Wolf said. He shook his son's limp body. "Answer me! Have you heard my words?"

There was no response. All was now quiet, except for the wind as it blew across the plains. One and then another of the warriors mounted up and rode away, leaving father and son alone.

With pensive eyes, Lone Wolf again looked at Swift Elk as he held him in his arms. A tear flowed down the creased, weathered face of the old Blackfoot Chief.

Removing his prized headdress of eagle feathers, Lone Wolf placed it on Swift Elk's head. "I have always been proud of you, my Son."

Swift Elk, struggling to open his eyes, looked up at his father.

"I have longed for this, Father," he said in a faint whisper, "to win your praise." His eyes filled with tears, then suddenly closed.

Lone Wolf pressed his son's body tightly against his own, and held him for a while. He felt the warmth slowly ebb.

The cry of an eagle once more pierced the silence. Lone Wolf looked up and watched as it flew off to the East.

Again, Lone Wolf prayed aloud to the Great Spirit:

"Had Swift Elk not heard my words, I would have done to him as my father did to me—failing to speak the words of praise a son longs to hear. Unlike my own, his soul will leave this world, unburdened."

Two young warriors, Swift Elk's closest friends, galloped over. Lone Wolf carried his son's body to them. Speaking only with their eyes, they took the body and tied it to Swift Elk's horse. They soon rode off, leaving Lone Wolf by himself.

When all were out of sight, Lone Wolf knelt and wept. He remained for a while, lost in the memories of a life long past. As the sun was about to set, he mounted his horse. Looking toward the western sky, he prayed one last time to the Great Spirit:

"You have taken my only son, but not before he heard the words of praise he sought since he was a boy. I would journey all my remaining days, Great Spirit, to hear the words my own father took to his grave, back in the Eastern Woodlands." Then, again, he heard the call of distant drums from out of the East. But there were no tribes to the East, not for more than three days ride by horse.

Lone Wolf rode off into the plains, spear in hand. He caught sight of the Great Buffalo on a distant ridge, silhouetted against the red and purple rays of the setting sun. The humped-back creature turned to look at Lone Wolf, then continued along its way into the horizon out of which it had first appeared.

Chapter 2

A Burial Robe

Mist settled over the snow-covered mountains surrounding the tribe's winter camp. A light rain began to fall in the wooded foothills below.

Swift Elk's body had been placed within the sacred lodge at the edge of Two Medicine Lake. Since morning, the tribal elders remained seated around the body, chanting prayers to safeguard Swift Elk's soul on its final journey to the Spirit Land. The sweet, pungent smoke of burning cedar, the breath of the Great Spirit, cast an eerie haze over all within the lodge. But Lone Wolf had yet to come.

"Where is our Chief?" Bird Rattler, the old gray-haired Medicine Man, asked the others again. "Lone Wolf knows well that the burial must take place before the sun sets this day!"

"I saw him ride from camp this past night," answered one of the tribal elders who had just joined the others. "He left, alone, after his son's body had been placed in the lodge, but has not been seen since."

"Lone Wolf must come soon," Bird Rattler said, "or we shall be forced to bury Swift Elk without the presence of his father. The sacred tradition of burial must not be broken, not even for a Warrior Chief. Evil fortune would befall our tribe, and Swift Elk's spirit placed in great peril."

The tribal elders shook their heads and grunted in agreement.

Bird Rattler and the elders went outside the medicine lodge. They waited anxiously for some sign of Lone Wolf. From time to time they looked up, straining their eyes through the mist to find the position of the sun.

"Perhaps some misfortune has already befallen our Chief," Bird Rattler said. "Perhaps in his grief he was foolish enough to challenge the Great Buffalo and, like his son, has become its victim."

Rain continued to fall, as the mist hanging over the surrounding mountains grew darker.

Suddenly, on the horizon, a man on horseback appeared. The distant figure followed the mountain trail leading from Cut Bank Pass, the main access to the nearby plains lying to the east.

They waited anxiously, without saying a word, until the figure of the lone rider became large enough to recognize.

"It is Dark Beaver, returning from a hunt," one of the young warriors finally called out.

"We can wait no longer!" Bird Rattler said. "The burial must take place before the sun sets, or we shall put Swift Elk's soul, and our own, in certain peril."

He motioned with his hand to two young warriors, Swift Elk's closest friends. They followed Bird Rattler back into the sacred lodge and, as directed by the old gray-haired Medicine Man, used the fur of a bighorn sheep to wrap Swift Elk's body, leaving only the eyes exposed. The body was carried out of the lodge, then tied securely to the two, long trailing poles of a travois which had been crossed and hitched over the back of Swift Elk's horse.

Stillness fell as the rain suddenly stopped. The surrounding mountains remained shrouded in mist.

The tribe, including women and children, assembled in the center of camp. Hides that covered the ceremonial ground were removed. The drums of the sacred burial dance began to beat. Warriors, wearing buffalo-horn headpieces, danced around Swift Elk's body. Their pounding footsteps created clouds of dust that enveloped each dancer like billows of smoke. The elders, seated around the outer circle, chanted a special prayer. "Oh, Great Spirit, we commend to you our brother, Swift Elk. May you deem his soul worthy to enter the Spirit Land."

As soon as the ceremonial dance was finished, the warriors mounted up. They pulled into a single line behind the horse-drawn travois, and began the procession to the tribal burial site. The women and children stood by and watched.

The procession left camp in silence, following the old path that winds its way along Cut Bank Creek. Each warrior carried his spear upright. The long line of mounted riders made its way through Cut Bank Pass, and into the adjoining woodland, dense with towering pines. They rode across the dark, needle-covered floor of the forest, where the fragrance of pine lingered like incense; then along the rugged foothills beyond; and finally up into the sacred mountain itself, the snow-covered Going-to-the-Sun-Mountain. There, high near its peak, was the ancient, sacred burial ground of the Blackfoot, known only to them.

The rocky path leading to the burial site above was barely wide enough for a horse to climb. Great caution had to be taken so that one's mount would not lose its footing on this cliff-edge trail, sending rider and horse to certain death on the crags below. Except for an occasional bighorn sheep that would pass from time to time, only the Blackfoot ever traveled this winding, hidden trail.

At the top of the trail was a level area, sheltered within a recess in the side of the mountain. The edge of this gravesite overlooked a deep precipice, while immediately above was the mountain peak, obscured in mist. The burial procession made its way into the level area. The warriors quickly dismounted, then gathered around two excavations, which had been dug in the rocky ground earlier that day.

Bird Rattler, anxious that the ceremony be completed before sunset, motioned again to the two young warriors, Swift Elk's closest friends. They untied the body and removed it from the cross poles of the travois.

As they were about to place the body into the open grave, the warriors in the burial party were startled by the sound of approaching hoof beats from the trail below. They reached for their spears, then waited for the intruder to come into sight. From around the bend a man on horseback appeared, followed by a packhorse.

"It is Lone Wolf!" Bird Rattler announced. "I am relieved that you are now here for the burial of your son, and without a moment to spare."

Lone Wolf raised his outstretched arm in greeting, but said nothing. He dismounted, walked to his packhorse, and untied rawhide lacing from around a large bundle. It fell to the ground.

With his back turned, he reached down and pulled out a large, heavy object. He grabbed it with both hands and, turning around, struggled to lift it above his head. The warriors gasped in disbelief as they stared at the head of the Great Buffalo.

"It was this beast that sent my only son to the Spirit Land," Lone Wolf said, with anger as well as sorrow in his voice. "And so shall its spirit escort my son there in tribute. The head of the Great Buffalo shall be buried with him."

The huge head was placed on the ground, alongside the open grave. Its large, blood red eyes seemed to follow the movements of each warrior.

Lone Wolf untied a second bundle from the packhorse, and took out the hide of a buffalo. He flung it outward with a violent, sweeping motion so that it unfurled over the ground for all to see its enormous size. The long fur glittered from the red and purple rays of the setting sun.

"And this shall be my son's burial robe, the only burial robe worthy of the chieftain he was to be, the fur of the animal he hunted last."

Lone Wolf turned to the two young warriors. "Remove the fur of the bighorn sheep, and wrap Swift Elk's body in this burial robe, as befits a Warrior Chief."

Noticing the rays of the sun beginning to fade, Bird Rattler urged the two warriors, "Hurry, his body must enter the grave while there is still light."

After Swift Elk had been wrapped in his new burial robe, he was lowered into the grave, facing west toward the setting sun. The head of the Great Buffalo was then placed into the grave at Swift Elk's feet, to accompany him on his journey to the Spirit Land.

Bird Rattler began to chant the concluding prayers of burial, as taught by tribal ancestors since the long ago. "May the Great Spirit take your soul, Swift Elk, and may He count you amongst his warriors of the eternal sun." He then motioned to all the warriors to file past for their final tribute.

Each warrior approached the open grave, then threw in one of his own arrows, marked with its distinctive feather pattern. "These arrows will be for you, Swift Elk, to use in the Spirit Land," Bird Rattler said, "when you once again take to the hunt."

After the travois had been unhitched from its back, Swift Elk's horse was led alongside the second excavation. Lone Wolf held the animal by its rawhide bridle, and stroked its neck gently to calm it. Bird Rattler pulled out a knife, and in the warrior tradition, quickly slit its throat. The horse that had accompanied Swift Elk throughout his earthly life would now accompany him to the Spirit Land, where they would again become companions of the hunt. As the heavy body of the animal began to collapse, it was pushed into the large grave immediately next to Swift Elk's.

Rocks and earth were then backfilled into both graves, and the ground surface leveled. Neither man nor animal would ever disturb these graves, for there was no trace as to what might lie below.

The burial ceremony was now finished. Bird Rattler motioned to all the warriors to mount up. He directed one of the elders to lead the procession down the narrow trail, back to the encampment below at Two Medicine Lake.

Soon the last rider disappeared behind the upper bend of the trail. Bird Rattler and Lone Wolf remained at the burial site.

"Are you not leaving, Bird Rattler?" Lone Wolf asked.

"No. I will stay here with you a while."

The two men sat quietly for a time alongside Swift Elk's grave. Bird Rattler placed his hand on Lone Wolf's shoulder, to console his friend of more than thirty snows. From the day Lone Wolf had first entered the camp of the Blackfoot, his adopted people, the two had remained close, with the elder Bird Rattler serving as Lone Wolf's mentor – and a second father of sorts.

There was a worried look on Bird Rattler's face and uneasiness in his voice when he finally broke the silence.

"Lone Wolf," he asked, "will not the killing of the Great Buffalo bring evil fortune upon our tribe? I fear that the creature's spirit may come back to haunt us. The buffalo herds would then no longer return to the upper plains, and our people would have no hunt."

"So that is why you have remained here with me," Lone Wolf said. "Fear not, for as you yourself have long taught, the spirit of any creature may be challenged when such is the will of the Great Spirit, as it was this past night."

"How can you be certain that this was so?" Bird Rattler asked.

Lone Wolf's thoughts returned to the night before, as he prepared to explain:

"My heart was heavy with grief," Lone Wolf began his story. "I rode into the plains, torch in hand, determined to pursue the creature that had taken my only son from me. I prayed to the Great Spirit to lead me through the dark to the place where I might find the Great Buffalo, and there confront it in battle. In such a challenge, one of us would surely perish. Now that my son had been taken from me, I would welcome death. And so, I eagerly set out to meet my fate, whatever it might be."

Bird Rattler moved closer to hear every word.

"As I rode across the plains, through the darkness," Lone Wolf continued, "I prayed for a sign to help find the place where the Great Buffalo goes to hide at night. The moment my torch burned out, I saw in the glow that now surrounded the moon such a sign. It was the white-headed eagle, circling overhead. It then flew toward the upper plains, in the direction of Redstone Canyon.

"And so I rode throughout the night, without stopping for rest, knowing I would surely find my destiny there, either as hunter or hunted.

"As I approached the canyon, I heard the panting of many buffalo, gathered closely together for the night, safe within the confines of this canyon-with-one-entrance. I realized that the Great Buffalo must be somewhere near the herd. But was he outside the canyon, or within? If within, he would be trapped, with no other opening from which to escape.

"I entered the mouth of the canyon. Blood surged through my veins. After riding only a short distance, the entire herd of buffalo charged toward me in a frenzied stampede. My horse and I would have both been trampled, if not for a protruding rock ledge, which we hid behind. As the long stream of buffalo rushed past, I watched carefully, hoping to find the Great Buffalo in their midst. But he was nowhere to be seen.

"It was then I knew that the cunning creature must still be inside the canyon, waiting for me to be trampled to death by the very stampede he had started.

"I rode deeper into the mouth of the canyon, my long spear pointed downward at the ready. All was quiet.

"When I was well within the canyon walls, the great beast suddenly came into view. He began to charge toward me. His huge head was bowed so that his sharp horns pointed upward toward the underbelly of my horse. His eyes were like glowing embers penetrating the dark, the crazed look of a demon rather than a creature of nature.

"My horse bravely held its ground until the very last. It reared up, and then came down with its front hooves striking the head of the creature, driving it backwards."

"The courage of your horse matches your own," Bird Rattler interrupted.

"My horse reared up once again," Lone Wolf continued. "I was thrown to the ground, where I lay dazed for a moment. My spear had fallen a short distance away, out of reach.

"The Great Buffalo, seeing me lying there helplessly, charged again. With head bowed low, it now pointed its sharp horns toward me.

"The creature closed in with incredible swiftness. I rolled over quickly and grabbed my spear.

"Still lying on the ground, I positioned my spearpoint upward, bracing the end of the shaft against the earth, knowing the great force that would be needed to pierce the hide of the crazed beast.

"As I was about to be gored by the charging buffalo, the spearpoint penetrated its body beneath the neck, and cut through its heart. I rolled over again quickly, just before the animal collapsed to the ground where I had been lying. Blood rushed from the mouth of the fallen beast, flowing into a pool that soaked the sandy ground red. The Great Buffalo's heavy panting grew weaker. Then it moved no more."

"To fell a creature such as this," Bird Rattler said, "requires the greatest courage and skill. You are, in truth, dear friend, a master of the hunt!"

"And so," Lone Wolf concluded his story, "it was clearly the will of the Great Spirit that not I, but rather the Great Buffalo should die. I had offered myself up freely and without reservation as I prayed that the will of the Great Spirit would reveal itself that night, in what could have been the last hunt of my earthly life."

"Indeed," Bird Rattler agreed, with a deep sigh of relief, "this must have been the will of the Great Spirit. It was so meant to be that you, Lone Wolf, should be the one to live. And in this I take great joy, that I shall continue to have my close friend of many snows, the respected and beloved Warrior Chief of our people. Only the bravest of men could have challenged the Great Buffalo in the manner you did — as a lone hunter without advantage, in the darkness of night. This story of your courageous deed will forever be told amongst the Blackfoot for as long as our campfires shall burn."

Bird Rattler again placed his hand on Lone Wolf's shoulder, this time in deep admiration for the great Warrior Chief, his closest friend.

"It is good, Bird Rattler," Lone Wolf said, "that having heard my story you are now relieved of your concern for the death of the Great Buffalo. But there is another matter of concern to me, one that has long burdened my heart, and which I now turn to you for your wise counsel."

"Yes, Lone Wolf, speak openly."

"I have never shared these thoughts with any man," Lone Wolf began, then hesitated a moment. "Before Swift Elk's death, I saw a vision of my long-dead father, appearing as he has from time to time. But, as always, he was silent."

"If my memory serves me," Bird Rattler said, "was he not the Chief of the people of your birth, in your ancestral lands back east?"

"Yes, it is that very matter that continues to haunt me, even after the many snows that have fallen since."

"How so, Lone Wolf?"

"Not long after I became a warrior, our village in the Eastern Woodlands was attacked by the treacherous white man, who set fire to our bark-covered lodges, the women and children trapped inside. My father, in his brave struggle to save them, was killed and so went to his grave before his time, taking with him those words I had longed to hear him speak: that I was worthy to succeed him as Warrior Chief of our people."

"But why," Bird Rattler questioned, "should this still be of concern, after the passage of so much time? Our people, who long since adopted you, have made you their own Warrior Chief. You alone command the three powerful tribes of the Blackfoot—the Siksika, the Piegan and the Blood. In all the lodges of our enemies in the Northern Plains, your name is spoken with awe. And you, as our fearless Chief, have kept the white man from our lands, having never lost in battle to the long swords. So why concern yourself now with what might have been in a time that is best forgotten?"

"My heart will not rest," Lone Wolf answered, "until it knows for certain what was in my father's own heart. For my brother, Rising Bear, a brother-of-the-same-birth, had competed against me for the honor of succeeding our father as Warrior Chief. Which of us would my father have chosen?"

"But now that he is dead, Lone Wolf, there is no good medicine that can resurrect your father from his grave, not even mine as powerful as it is."

"How, then, can I find the truth, in that the vision of my father refuses to speak?"

Bird Rattler sat quietly for a while, his eyes fixed in deep thought. "Yes, then," Bird Rattler finally answered, "you must seek out the Great Spirit. He alone commands both the living and the dead, for He is Chief of all those that dwell in this world, and of all the people

16

of the past. He can send your father to you, with words that will set your spirit free."

"A vision quest of the Great Spirit, then?" Lone Wolf asked.

"That is the only way. And you need not travel far, for it is here on this sacred mountain that the Great Spirit dwells, as He has since the beginning of time."

"Then I shall remain here," Lone Wolf said, "and seek Him out."

"But I must caution you, Lone Wolf," Bird Rattler warned. "There may be other matters that lie buried within your heart that you cannot hide from the Great Spirit, for He knows the innermost, darkest thoughts of us all."

Bird Rattler placed his hand on Lone Wolf's shoulder one last time to bid farewell. He mounted up and rode down the winding trail, capturing the last rays of the setting sun.

Lone Wolf remained behind at the burial site, alone. He would seek a vision from the Great Spirit who, the Blackfoot believed, had always dwelt here on this sacred mountain. And not even Bird Rattler's ominous warning could deter Lone Wolf from confronting the Great Spirit, now that He had taken his only son from him.

Kneeling over Swift Elk's grave, Lone Wolf prayed. All around him mist began to close in, a bone-chilling mist that had settled from the ancient peak hidden above.

Chapter 3

Seeking a Vision

Throughout the night, Lone Wolf kept vigil over the grave of his son, high on the sacred mountain. A sense of disbelief came over him. Swift Elk's death must surely have been a dream. Lone Wolf would soon awake and, once again, hear his son's familiar voice.

But there, alongside, was the fresh grave.

Lone Wolf walked over to a nearby rock ledge. He stood for a while at the very edge. Throughout his life, with all its ordeals, he had never felt such anguish. How easy it would be to end it all, there on the crags below.

"Great Spirit," Lone Wolf called out, "how could You allow this to happen—having to bury my only son? Why was it not me, instead, now that I am nearing the end of my life?" Lone Wolf removed the fur from around him. The night air sent chills through his body.

"Until my death, Great Spirit, sorrow shall be my constant companion."

Lone Wolf realized he was far from ready to return to his tribe, if indeed he could ever return at all. He would remain alone in this remote, sacred place, with its ancient graves of the Blackfoot, and the fresh grave of his son. For it was here on Going-to-the-Sun-Mountain, that the Blackfoot believed the Great Spirit dwelt. During the following days and nights, he would pray and fast. The earthly matters of food and sleep were now of no concern. He would not leave until he had been sent a vision from the Great Spirit!

Again, Lone Wolf called out into the black of night. "Why, Great Spirit, did you take my son from me, like my father before him, both before their time?"

All was silent.

Throughout the night, Lone Wolf continued to call out to the Great Spirit, that He might reveal Himself, or send an omen. He clutched his good medicine, raising the small buckskin pouch toward the sky as he prayed.

Still there was no answer.

The dawn found Lone Wolf wide-awake, and again perched precariously atop the rock ledge that overlooked the lower mountain range. The world below was blanketed in mist, except for a few snow-covered peaks penetrating through, giving one the sense of being adrift high above the clouds.

The rays of the sun finally reached the ledge, bringing warmth to Lone Wolf's chilled body. Throughout the day he continued to pray aloud and to beseech the Great Spirit to answer his vision quest. But again all was silent.

As he looked up to the mountain peak overhead, Lone Wolf cried out, "Great Spirit, how could You allow such a tragedy to befall Swift Elk, who always did your will, while others are left in this world to do evil? And why have You taken them all from me, the ones I had loved? Father, mother, wife, and now my son—for each an early death that inflicted more anguish on my grieved spirit? For what reason do You forever test me, even now that I am nearing the end of my life? Have I not proven myself, Father of all spirits, proven my courage as a warrior many times before?"

"Speak to me!" Lone Wolf continued to cry out, as his sorrow and anger grew. "Show your face to your faithful warrior who has always believed in you. And tell me, I beg, what was in my father's heart, before you took him from me."

All was quiet, except for the wind.

***

The sun began to set for a second night. Lone Wolf continued to pray for a vision, while fighting off the sleep his body craved. Darkness fell.

"Do you, indeed, even exist, Great Spirit?" he shouted with all the fury he could summon from his exhausted body. His words echoed from the surrounding mountains. "Are the long-held beliefs, passed onto us by our ancestors, not true? Could it be there is no Great Spirit? If you exist, why will you not reveal yourself, once and for all?"

But again all was quiet, except for the wind.

***

Lone Wolf remained awake throughout the night. In early morning a light rain began to fall. The wetness sent his near-frozen body into shivers.

He walked over to the nearby rock ledge and, standing at the very edge, cried out to the Great Spirit, one last time:

"Father of all spirits, why have You forsaken me?"

Suddenly a strong wind blew down from the ancient peak, driving Lone Wolf back from the edge of the cliff. He collapsed from exhaustion onto the ground, alongside the grave of his son. Immediately he fell into a deep sleep that lasted throughout the day and into the third and final eve of his vigil.

In a dream, Lone Wolf saw his son Swift Elk, as a young boy, in the woods near Two Medicine Lake. There, too, he saw himself as a young man, teaching his son to hunt, as his own father had once taught him. Swift Elk looked up and smiled, with the fleeting innocence of a child. The air was filled with the fragrance of the surrounding pines. The sky was bright blue.

All seemed at peace on that summer day long past, just an ordinary day that until now had been lost in memory. If only Lone Wolf could return, even for a moment...to embrace his son one last time.

Slowly, the images faded. But the Spirit of Dreams had not yet finished with him.

Lone Wolf, lying on the ground, remained in a deep sleep. His mind now traveled back further in time to a distant land, a land far from the Northern Plains of the Blackfoot.

He saw himself as a youth, wearing the single-feather head roach of a warrior, recently won. On the hunt with his father, he made his way through the hills of the Eastern Woodlands, tribal grounds of the Weckquasgeek, the people of his birth.

Young Lone Wolf aimed his bow at a hawk perched within the canopy of a tall oak. As he let loose his arrow, the bird flew off to a higher limb.

Lone Wolf's father, Gray Eagle, stood nearby. "Try again, quickly, before your prey has time to take cover."

Again Lone Wolf pulled back on the tight sinew of his powerful bow and, with hands shaking, released the arrow. It shot between the branches of the tree, slashing through the thick leaves until it embedded itself beneath the limb where the hawk had been perched.

No sooner had the bird flown to a nearby tree, than Gray Eagle turned quickly and let loose an arrow of his own. Its slender quartz point pierced the breast of the elusive bird, coming out through its back. The hawk was swept from its perch, then fell between the tree limbs, landing on the leaf-covered ground.

"You are a great hunter!" young Lone Wolf called out, in admiration of the father he had always adored.

Gray Eagle put down his bow and placed his hand on his son's shoulder. "You, too, must learn to release your arrow without delay," he counseled young Lone Wolf. "Never allow your prey, nor your enemy, any chance to take cover. Always strike quickly. This, and courage, are the most important traits of a hunter and warrior. Like the wolf, your namesake, pursue your prey with utmost swiftness."

"Father, do you think some day I, too, may acquire such skills, required of a Warrior Chief?"

Gray Eagle answered deliberately, with words that Lone Wolf would carry with him for the rest of his life.

"You must first prove yourself beyond question, my son. You must show yourself worthy of such an honor by your skills on the hunt and your bravery in battle, above that of any warrior. There are those in this tribe, including your own brother, who may challenge you one day in your bid to succeed me as Warrior Chief. Our people will not make you their Chief merely because you are my son. You must prove yourself, time and again, on the hunt and in battle, so there is no doubt at all in the minds of our people, nor in mine."

And so were spoken the words that would haunt Lone Wolf for the rest of his life, and that would forever drive him in his relentless pursuit of glory. What, then, must he do to prove himself to his people, and especially to his father? What great act of courage was necessary to prove himself 'beyond question,' so that his father would bestow upon him, rather than on his brother, the coveted headdress of Warrior Chief? The answer he would seek out during the many battles that lay ahead. And like his search for the Great Spirit, the truth would forever elude him, until finally revealing itself in a manner least expected.

With the words of his long-dead father echoing in his mind, Lone Wolf awoke from his sleep. It was late in the day. Though faint from his fasting, he could remember all that he had dreamt, of times long past. But what was their meaning? Was this the vision that he had sought from the Great Spirit, or perhaps part of it?

As he struggled to get to his feet, Lone Wolf nearly collapsed from the stiffness in his legs. He walked cautiously toward the ledge. The mist that had obscured the peak of the sacred mountain had finally lifted.

Just then, he heard the piercing cry of a bird. Lone Wolf looked up. He saw a white-headed eagle soaring above the snow- covered peak. The eagle circled three times, then flew off toward the plains. The eagle returned. Again it circled overhead, then flew to the east.

An omen! This must be the very sign he had sought from the Great Spirit on his vision quest, Lone Wolf thought. Was the white-headed eagle, like the distant drums he had heard from time to time throughout his life, now calling him to return to his ancestral lands in the East? Bird Rattler, the old gray-haired Medicine Man, and the wisest of all in such matters, could confirm this for him.

Lone Wolf walked over to the hidden grave of his son and, kneeling down, whispered a final prayer:

"I will join you in the Spirit Land, Swift Elk, after my own life is done. And there, we shall once again take to the hunt."

Glancing back at the grave for the last time, Lone Wolf left the ridge on foot, and headed down the steep mountain trail. Not far below, just beyond the bend, he found his horse feeding on shrubs growing in a rock crevice. Lone Wolf called out to the pinto, Wacanga, his loyal companion of many snows. His horse neighed and came over to him. Patting its brown and white face, he mounted up and slowly rode down the narrow trail.

When he finally reached the valley below, Lone Wolf paused to look back at the snow-covered peak of Going-to-the-Sun Mountain. Could it be, he wondered, that the Great Spirit did not dwell there at all, despite the legends of the Blackfoot?

Lone Wolf recalled a story he had heard as a child. It was back in the land of his birth, in the Eastern Woodlands, that the Great Spirit dwelt. It was there, at the cliffs which towered above the Mahikanittuc River, that He lay down to rests each night. Then, again, Lone Wolf heard distant drums from out of the East.

As the rays of the sun disappeared below the mountains, Lone Wolf pushed his horse into a gallop. When he returned to the camp of the Blackfoot, all had retired to their lodges. He would have to wait until morning before he could seek out Bird Rattler.

Chapter 4

His Adopted People

The morning after his return to camp, Lone Wolf went in search of his old friend Bird Rattler. No doubt, he would be able to interpret the omen Lone Wolf had seen on his vision quest. He found the venerable Medicine Man in his lodge, seated with the elders beside the fire. The sweet smell of tobacco filled the lodge as they passed around the long-stem pipe. Greeting Lone Wolf warmly, the men were relieved to see him return safely, and eager to hear of his vision quest.

Sitting down alongside Bird Rattler, Lone Wolf lost no time in recounting the story of his three-day ordeal on the sacred mountain. He told of the omen he had seen on the final day, of the white-headed eagle circling above the snow-covered peak, then flying east.

Bird Rattler immediately dropped the pipe he was smoking. A worried look came over his face. He fumbled about, before picking up the burning pipe from the furs that lined the floor of the lodge.

Lone Wolf waited for Bird Rattler to regain his composure then asked him the meaning of the omen.

Bird Rattler, after a long silence, finally spoke. "For a sign such as this, I will have to consult the spirits to know for certain. This requires time, Lone Wolf, so you must be patient. But for now, take this which we have prepared for you."

Lone Wolf was handed a wooden bowl containing the traditional drink taken after a vision quest. Made from roots and bark, its healing powers quickly began to restore his strength. After finishing the potion, the long-stem pipe was passed to him. He inhaled deeply of the aromatic smoke, putting him immediately at ease.

"Before you entered the lodge, Lone Wolf," one of the elders said, "we were once again telling stories. Now it is Bird Rattler's turn. Let us hear from him another of his wondrous tales."

Bird Rattler nodded his head then, to Lone Wolf's surprise, began recounting stories of Lone Wolf's own exploits among the Blackfoot.

Perhaps he already knew the meaning of the omen, Lone Wolf thought.

"Seeing Lone Wolf return here today," Bird Rattler began, "reminded me of the first time I laid eyes on him. On that fateful day, long ago, Lone Wolf rode from the plains and onto our lands, not knowing where he was."

"Nor what awaited me," Lone Wolf interrupted.

"He had been a fugitive," Bird Rattler continued, "fleeing from the white man's reservation, in the region where the tribe of the Oklahoma once ruled."

"I was the first of our people to see the stranger. I had been out alone when I caught sight of him riding from the east, along Cut Bank Creek. He was dressed in a manner unknown to us. I rushed back to camp and called out the warriors to greet him, since he was not of our people, nor of any tribes of the plains."

"Greet me?" Lone Wolf interrupted again. "Attack me is more the truth."

Bird Rattler smiled. "You know the Blackfoot allow no one to pass through our lands without our consent. Is this not so, Lone Wolf?"

"This is so," he answered. "But was it necessary to send so many warriors against one lone rider?"

"Had I known it was you, Lone Wolf, and known then of your fierceness as a warrior, I would surely have sent twice that number!"

The elders all laughed.

"And so it was," Bird Rattler continued, "that Lone Wolf first entered into our lands, having ridden a great distance to outrun the bluecoat horse soldiers who had been in pursuit."

"He asked to stay a while amongst our people, and being of an Algonquin tongue, we honored his request. None of us knew at that time he would become one of us, and never leave.

"Before the next snow, this newcomer called Lone Wolf would prove his courage by a feat of bravery that has long since become tribal lore, and which I recount to you now.

"Our Chief at the time, Red Hawk, during the summer-of-little-rain, had formed a raiding party to recover horses from the Kutenai. They had been seen crossing onto our side of the mountains, hunting for the wild horses of the plains that belong to our people. Five of our warriors, led by Chief Red Hawk, made their way to the Kutenai camp that lies on the west slope of the mountains.

"Lone Wolf, not yet of our tribe, followed to the rear of our mounted warriors. They rode up through Glacier Pass, where the snow never melts, then into the Rocky Mountains beyond.

"When they reached a sharp bend in the trail, they were attacked by a Kutenai war party lying in ambush. Having the advantages of surprise and high ground, the Kutenai made short work of massacring our warriors.

"While this was happening, Lone Wolf had lagged behind, stopping to remove a stone wedged in the hoof of his horse. When he finally approached the area of the ambush, he dismounted and took cover.

"As the Kutenai were leaving, he noticed our Chief had been taken captive and his hands tied behind his back as he rode. Lone Wolf followed at a safe distance. The war party stopped before sunset, making camp for the night rather than risk traveling down the steep trail during fading light.

"After tying our Chief to a tree, they prepared their food, not realizing they had been followed. When dark had fallen, Lone Wolf crept quietly to the edge of the

27

camp. He made quick work of a warrior standing watch, dragging him into the thick underbrush. Four others remained.

"One of the warriors, hearing the rustling within the bushes, went to investigate. He met a similar fate. The others were now alerted.

"Lone Wolf mounted up quickly. Before the Kutenai could get to their horses, he charged into the midst of the three remaining warriors.

"The nearest Kutenai attempted to knock Lone Wolf from his horse, but instead, was kicked to the ground. He struck his head against a rock and was heard from no more.

"Another rushed Lone Wolf from the opposite side. Lone Wolf swung his spear point around. The warrior was impaled.

"The last remaining Kutenai, youngest of the war party, froze in his tracks.

"Lone Wolf ordered him, 'Release my Chief at once, or you will meet your end right where you stand!'

"The young brave obeyed without delay, rushing over to the tree and untying our Chief, who had witnessed all.

"From the vantage of his horse, Lone Wolf motioned to the trembling Kutenai to approach him. The young brave looked up at Lone Wolf, expecting the worst.

"'I will spare your life, so that you may return to your people to tell them of all that has happened. And warn them, as well, that they are never again to enter the lands of the Blackfoot. The wild horses and buffalo that roam on the eastern side of these mountains belong to the Blackfoot alone.'

"Lone Wolf and our Chief then rode off, taking all the horses with them. The young Kutenai fled on foot.

"As soon as they returned to camp," Bird Rattler continued, "Chief Red Hawk summoned all the tribe together and, standing outside his lodge, recounted this same story for all to hear."

"'The likes of such bravery I have never seen,' the Chief finished his story, with Lone Wolf at his side. 'This newcomer, this stranger amongst us, single-handedly saved my life without regard for his own. He is a true warrior.'

"With all the tribe watching, our Chief took off the breast beads that he wore, those with the insignia of a charging buffalo. He presented them to Lone Wolf who immediately put them on.

"'You, Lone Wolf,' the Chief pronounced, 'now belong to the Blackfoot-Blood of the Northern Plains. From this day, forever, we shall count you as our own.'

"He then took Lone Wolf's right hand. Using a stone knife, he made a slit within Lone Wolf's palm and, in turn, a slit in his own. Clasping the two bloodied hands together and raising them above their heads, Red Hawk said for all to hear:

"Your Chief, who has for all this time gone without a son of his own, declares that from this day Lone Wolf shall be my adopted son, my blood now running in his veins and his blood in mine.'"

"And so it was," Bird Rattler concluded his story, "that good fortune befell our tribe when Lone Wolf first entered our land, and soon became one of us."

***

The long-stem pipe was passed again to Bird Rattler, who drew from it a deep breath of the aromatic smoke. Being the revered Medicine Man that he was, the elders seated within the lodge conceded to him the privilege of continuing his story-telling.

"Soon after," Bird Rattler began his next story, "Lone Wolf settled into a happy life here amongst us."

"One day he set out on foot, on the hunt for fresh meat. He was determined to track a buck, the largest ever seen in these forests. He knew that from time to time the cautious animal would come down to the lake, to drink and to feed on the tender grasses that grew along its banks.

29

"Since early morning he had been following the tracks of the buck deep within the forest. As the animal made its way through the trees and toward the edge of the woods that surrounded the lake, Lone Wolf lost sight of it. He crouched down in the undergrowth and remained motionless, listening for the slightest sound that might give away the location of his prey. At that moment, he heard rustling coming from the tall grasses that grew within the clearing between the edge of the forest and the lake.

"Like the wise hunter that he is," Bird Rattler continued, "Lone Wolf sprang to his feet, then charged into the clearing, his spear ready for the kill."

"And quite a kill it was!" Bird Rattler laughed. "What strange prey should now confront this brave new warrior of the Blackfoot? With spear in hand ready to strike, he encountered the most beautiful of Indian maidens, just then coming out of the water from bathing, without benefit of any clothing."

The elders all laughed.

"She screamed upon seeing Lone Wolf charging out of the brush like a crazed madman. When his eyes caught sight of her beautiful figure, Lone Wolf froze in his tracks. The maiden quickly took modest refuge by crouching low within the tall grass, lest this warrior lose even more of his wits. Our brave Lone Wolf then fled, without so much as a farewell to this young beauty."

Again the elders laughed, as Lone Wolf joined in.

"So it was that Lone Wolf, within days of saving the life of our old Chief, met his only daughter in this most unusual way.

"Lone Wolf," Bird Rattler concluded his story, "went on to marry this woman-of-the-lake, called Spring Woman, the daughter of our Chief. And so Lone Wolf became both the Chief's adopted son and son-in-marriage."

"Just after the first snow, she bore him a fine son, our beloved Swift Elk, who now hunts far beyond in the Spirit Land."

The rest of the story of Spring Woman was not told by Bird Rattler. It would have been too painful for Lone Wolf to hear, especially after having just buried his son.

But the memories returned, forcing their way into Lone Wolf's thoughts once the name of Spring Woman had been spoken. As he sat there in the lodge amongst the elders, he no longer heard the words being said aloud. Instead the memories of Spring Woman returned, memories he had long tried to forget:

She had been carrying water to the lodge on that fateful day in late fall, when a bearded white man, a fur trader, rode into camp. After dismounting, the fur trader pulled out of the bundle on his packhorse an assortment of knives made of the white man's gleaming metal—'the stone that never breaks.' He arranged them on a blanket spread over the ground. The men of the tribe had been out hunting, and the women in the camp were at first reluctant to approach the stranger. The fur trader kept motioning to them to come over to examine his wares. Finally, they approached cautiously, one by one. Spring Woman soon followed and was attracted by a gleaming hunting knife with a leather-wrapped handle. She went back to her lodge and got a beautiful otter skin which Lone Wolf had given her as a gift. Upon returning, she traded the skin for the metal hunting knife to give to Lone Wolf.

No sooner had the bartering been completed, than Lone Wolf rode back toward camp. He had never before seen a white man within the lands of the Blackfoot. Watching from a distance, Lone Wolf felt growing rage as the fur trader urged the women to bring out as many furs as they could to exchange for his goods. He

31

remained hidden, waiting for the fur trader to complete his bartering.

As the white intruder loaded up his furs and prepared to ride out of camp, Lone Wolf galloped over and snatched the reins of his horse. With one slash of his stone knife, Lone Wolf cut the rawhide lacing used to secure the large bundle of furs to the back of the trailing pack horse. The bundle fell to the ground.

Fire raged in Lone Wolf's eyes as he spoke to the intruder. "Never again enter the lands of the Blackfoot, not even to pass!"

The fur trader attempted to answer, but broke into a raspy cough.

"I warn you one last time," Lone Wolf said before the fur trader could regain his voice, "No white man may enter upon the lands of the Blackfoot, for any reason. Return no more, for if you do, I shall kill you upon sight!"

The white man nodded and, kicking his horse repeatedly, galloped out of camp, leaving all his bartered furs lying on the ground where they had fallen.

"Why have you done this, my husband?" Spring Woman asked.

"The white man, like all of his kind, is treacherous," Lone Wolf replied. "First they come to barter for furs, then they will want our tribal lands."

"But how do you know this?" Spring Woman asked.

Lone Wolf explained what had happened to his own people, back in the Eastern Woodlands of his birth, how they had been cheated, first out of their furs, then out of their ancestral lands. He warned that if the Blackfoot were ever to allow the white man to enter into the Northern Plains, the same fate would befall them.

When he seemed to have calmed, Spring Woman handed Lone Wolf the hunting knife she had received just moments before. Its long, sharp blade gleamed from the rays of the afternoon sun.

"No," Lone Wolf said, refusing to even touch the knife.

"Why, Lone Wolf?" she asked, tearfully.

"My love for you is as great as that any man has felt for a woman. But my hatred of the white man, whose treachery I have known since youth, is so deep that I cannot accept anything from his hands. I would be reminded of things I have long sought to forget."

"A true hunter," Lone Wolf continued, "should make with his own hands all things that he needs, as has always been our way."

Later that day they went down together to Two Medicine Lake, into which Spring Woman threw the white man's knife.

A short time after this incident, Spring Woman contracted a strange cough, not responsive to Bird Rattler's special medicines. The strange cough until that time was unknown to the Blackfoot, and was like the cough of the white fur trader who had visited the camp.

Before the next moon, Spring Woman died from what came to be called 'the white man's coughing sickness.' Lone Wolf wept bitterly for the loss of the woman he loved, the mother of young Swift Elk, and the only woman that he would ever take as wife throughout his life.

Lone Wolf's hatred for the white man grew deeper. He vowed openly to all the Blackfoot warriors that he would kill on sight any white man who dared enter their lands.

Soon after Spring Woman's death, as Bird Rattler was about to recount in his own storytelling, Lone Wolf would become the Warrior Chief of the Blackfoot. His first act as Chief would be to summon together the three powerful tribes of the Blackfoot Nation: the Siksika, the Piegan, and the Blood.

They all gathered on the Northern Plains just beyond Buffalo Cliffs. There they were addressed by Lone Wolf, mounted on his horse, wearing his eagle-feathered war bonnet. Streaks of red-earthen war paint covered his face.

"Warriors of the Blackfoot Nation, masters of the Northern Plains, heed well my words, for only in this way will we survive as a people. From this day, forever, we banish the white man from entering upon our sacred lands."

During those thirty snows that Lone Wolf ruled as Warrior Chief, his decree was enforced without exception, and the Blackfoot remained the most feared tribe of the Northern Plains.

***

Lone Wolf's thoughts returned to the present as he heard Bird Rattler's voice, once again offering him the long-stem pipe. He inhaled the soothing smoke, then passed the pipe to the elder seated beside him.

Bird Rattler noticed the elders were now becoming restless. "Let me end my storytelling," he said, "with a final episode in Lone Wolf's extraordinary life here amongst the Blackfoot."

"During the spring that followed the-winter-of-drifting-snows," Bird Rattler continued, "Chief Red Hawk died of old age. No sooner did the Great Spirit take him from us, than Lone Wolf summoned all the tribe to assemble in the center of camp. Once they had gathered, Lone Wolf came out of his lodge, holding the Chief's eagle-feathered war bonnet in one hand and a spear in the other.

"'Our Warrior Chief has passed over to the Spirit Land,' Lone Wolf announced. 'The custom of our people is that upon the death of a chief, his son shall succeed him. I am that son.'

"'I claim the title of Warrior Chief not by such custom of succession. I claim it solely as a hunter and warrior.'

"There was a surge of whispering amongst the tribe. 'What did he mean by this?'

"'Any warrior bold enough to challenge,' Lone Wolf said, 'may wear this headdress of Warrior Chief, should he prove himself worthy.'

"No sooner had he spoken these words, than Lone Wolf lifted his spear high above his head and threw it a short distance. The stone point disappeared beneath the surface of the ground. He walked over and placed the coveted war bonnet onto the end of the angled shaft. He then motioned to all the warriors with open palm.

"One young warrior took a step forward. Lone Wolf immediately pulled out his stone knife, and holding it outstretched, pointed it toward the challenger. The meaning was clear to all. Whoever dared to claim this trophy of battle must first do battle with Lone Wolf. And as all the warriors who had ridden with him knew, Lone Wolf would fight to his death.

"The challenger neared the war bonnet and went to grab his own knife. He froze in his tracks, seeing the crazed look in Lone Wolf's eyes, like that of a wild grizzly about to attack. The challenger slowly stepped backward, realizing he was no match for Lone Wolf, nor was any other warrior of our tribe."

Bird Rattler continued with his final story. "Seeing that there were now no other challengers, I took it upon myself, as Medicine Man, to walk over to where the war bonnet rested on the end of the spear. I made my way slowly ...and nervously."

The elders seated in the lodge laughed. Lone Wolf joined in.

"I removed the war bonnet and, turning toward all those gathered, announced:

"'Lone Wolf, since becoming one of us, has proven himself worthy to lead our people, by virtue of his loyalty to those who have led us before, and his unfailing courage in battle. He has also proven his honor, as at this moment when he could have claimed the

Chieftaincy by succession, long our custom, choosing instead to allow for open challenge.'

"'This is a true warrior, a man of courage and honor, one who deserves to lead the Blackfoot, and to wear this prized headdress.'

"'On behalf of our people, I declare Lone Wolf to be the Warrior Chief of the Blackfoot.'

"The eagle-feathered war bonnet I then placed on his head.

"At that moment, the tribe gave shouts of approval, including the warrior who only moments before had foolishly challenged Lone Wolf. "

***

"And so, my friend," Bird Rattler concluded his chronicle of Lone Wolf's life among the Blackfoot, "it was the will of the Great Spirit that He led you here, far from your ancestral lands in the East. His providence was that you would find your way to us, rather than to one of our enemies through whose lands you first passed. For here you would become the greatest of all Warrior Chiefs ever to lead the Blackfoot, winning the respect and love of your adopted people."

All those seated around the fire shook their heads and grunted in agreement.

Now that Bird Rattler had finished at long last, the elders wasted no time in excusing themselves, heading straight toward the smell of buffalo stew simmering outside. Lone Wolf and Bird Rattler remained alone in the lodge.

"Lone Wolf," Bird Rattler began, "do these stories not tell of the wonderful life you have had here among the Blackfoot?"

"You know already," Lone Wolf asked, "the meaning of the omen?"

"Yes, I fear there is little doubt," Bird Rattler answered, now with sorrow in his voice.

"You must understand," Lone Wolf explained. "I have grown old since I first entered these lands, and my strength lessens with each passing day. If I do not begin this journey soon, I will never be able to return to the land of my birth."

"But we are now your people, Lone Wolf. Your life for over thirty snows has been here among the Blackfoot, where the Great Spirit led you long ago."

"Yes, this is difficult," Lone Wolf brooded. "Very difficult."

"And remember, Lone Wolf, that the Blackfoot are masters of the Northern Plains, where the white man dares not enter. As you yourself have said, the white man now rules the Eastern Woodlands of your birth. Would you not put your freedom, your life, in great peril were you to return?"

"Perhaps, but my soul will not rest until I have seen for one last time the Sacred Cliffs of my ancestral lands, and have sought out the Great Spirit who dwells there. He alone can tell me what was in my father's heart before he died."

"Sleep on this, Lone Wolf," Bird Rattler said. "You may see yet another vision in your dreams and decide to remain here with us, after all. For this I pray."

Lone Wolf placed his hand on Bird Rattler's shoulder for a moment, without speaking, then returned to his own lodge.

As he walked back, he thought of how much easier it would be to remain here among the Blackfoot and his close friend, Bird Rattler. But then, his life was quickly passing, and he must decide soon, while he still had strength left to endure a long journey.

Chapter 5

"I Will Hunt the Buffalo No More"

Lone Wolf returned to his lodge for the night. Exhaustion overwhelming him at last, he lay down and wrapped himself in a buffalo fur. How lonely the lodge was, without Swift Elk. The mat on which his son would have lain was empty. For a moment he saw there the specter of Swift Elk, as a child, asleep near those he loved.

In the area next to his own was the place where Spring Woman would have slept, sharing with Lone Wolf each other's body warmth during the long winter nights. Now they were both gone, son and wife, passed on to the Spirit Land. Yet, Lone Wolf was still here.

He had trouble falling asleep. Images began to flash through his mind, of the mountains and plains, and of his exploits among the Blackfoot. But how could he remain in this land to live out his life, as Bird Rattler pleaded, now that he had no family left?

Lone Wolf at long last fell asleep. As he dreamt, his mind drifted back in time:

There, sitting around the fire within the lodge, were the three of them: Lone Wolf, Spring Woman and their son, Swift Elk, then only a boy. It was winter, and outside a deep show covered the ground. Inside, the buffalo-hide tepee was warm and comfortable as the flames of the evening fire cast soft glows over their faces.

Spring Woman was busy making winter clothing. She had sewn together pieces of buckskin with strips of sinews taken from the leg muscle of a deer. Her agile hands were now inserting porcupine quills into the hide. The quills had been dyed different colors for decorating the buckskin jacket she was fashioning for Lone Wolf.

She looked up for a moment and smiled as her eyes caught Lone Wolf's.

Lone Wolf smiled, in turn, then continued making a stone spearpoint for Swift Elk, all the while explaining to his young son the techniques involved. Holding a large piece of flint against a flat rock, he struck it with another stone. As he chipped away fragments, the long, tapered point began to take shape. Lone Wolf, now using a tool made from a deer antler, carefully applied pressure along the edges of the stone point, removing small flakes to create sharp serrations on each side. Young Swift Elk watched intently as his father's skilled hands completed the black-sheen spearpoint.

Lone Wolf handed the finished piece to Swift Elk to feel its sharpness. "A spearpoint such as this," he said, "would surely have brought down a woolly mammoth."

"Father, what is a woolly mammoth" young Swift Elk asked. "What does it look like?"

"The woolly mammoth was the largest of animals," Lone Wolf explained, "an animal that once lived in the Eastern Woodlands of my birth."

The images within the buffalo-hide tepee began to slowly fade.

As Lone Wolf slept, his mind drifted back further in time, to his ancestral lands in the East, and to a different lodge:

There around the fire was Lone Wolf, then only a boy, sitting within the bark-covered wigwam. There, too, was his mother, Sun Woman; his brother, Rising Bear; and his father, Gray Eagle, Warrior Chief of the Weckquasgeek.

Young Lone Wolf and his brother waited anxiously for their father to tell another of his stories, as he often did after the evening meal.

"This is the most important of all our legends," Gray Eagle began, "that of the origin of our tribe:

"In the long ago, when ice covered much of the land, only the animals lived here. There were no people.

"One day, after a heavy snow, a group of nomadic hunters dressed in bear skins, wandered for the first time into this valley we now call our own. They were on the hunt, in search of the elk and caribou that had disappeared from their own lands. The wolves, which they kept with them for tracking prey, had led them over a great distance. Here, in the valley of the Mahikanittuc River, they found the prey they sought, and another animal, the likes of which they had never seen before, the great woolly mammoth—a huge, four-legged beast, with long, brown fur and two upcurved tusks that wrapped back around each other. This creature was as high as three warriors standing on each other's shoulders. Upon first seeing one, the hunters were terrified and stayed far away. Nor did they move their camp into the valley, in fear of these enormous animals that made the ground shake whenever they walked.

"From time to time the hunters returned to the valley in search of prey. They eventually became familiar with the sight and habits of the mammoths. The woolly beasts would feed at the foot of the glaciers where melting ice made the ground plants grow thick. Whenever the hunters came within sight of a mammoth, it would give out with a thunderous roar through its long nose, which resembled the trunk of a tree. The sound would echo off the surrounding glaciers, sending chills up the spine of all that heard it.

"A lone hunter from this group, one day while tracking an elk, lost his footing on the surface of a glacier. He slid down the icy slope and, unable to catch himself, landed at the feet of a mammoth. Lying on his back, he looked up at the startled beast, which let out a deafening roar. The hunter quickly got up off the ground to avoid being stepped on. Grabbing his long spear, he jabbed its stone point toward the animal's underbelly.

"As the mammoth moved forward, the sharp point pierced its woolly hide. The beast stopped, then again, let out an earsplitting roar. Blood began to drip out of its wound. The hunter jabbed a second time at the enraged animal. The mammoth attempted to charge. The hunter stepped back then lunged forward, jabbing repeatedly with his long spear.

"The battle continued for a while, the blood of the weakened mammoth now spilling out of numerous wounds onto the snow. Suddenly its heavy bulk collapsed, causing the earth to shake. The hunter quickly climbed onto the furry mound of the fallen animal. He stabbed again and again into its neck, until the mammoth stopped breathing.

"Splattered with blood, the hunter went out to find the others of his group. He led them back to the kill. They cautiously approached the huge, lifeless body lying at the foot of the glacier. Its blood had stained the snow red. They could feel the warmth radiating from the long-haired beast. One and then another of the hunters climbed on top of the fallen animal. Standing together on the mound of flesh, they raised their spears above their heads.

"'We will pray to the spirit of this woolly mammoth,' the hunter addressed his group, 'so that from this day we may hunt its kind and always find food enough to feed our people.'

"No sooner had they climbed off the mammoth, then they were struck with awe. The field of snow that surrounded them took on a crimson glow. It seemed as though the blood of the fallen beast continued to flow, spreading slowly outward until it covered all the earth.

"'Look beyond!' the hunter called out to the others, pointing with his outstretched spear toward the western sky. There on the distant shore was the sun, ablaze in crimson and gold, setting atop the cliffs that towered above the river. Kneeling down, the hunters buried their spear points into the snow. They watched in silence as the sun sank below the distant cliffs, lying down to rest within its ancient stone lodge.

"The hunter turned toward the others and said:

"'This is the sign for which our people have long searched. It is here, in this valley, that we have found the animals needed to sustain our tribe. And it is here, at the sacred cliffs beyond, that we have found the very place where the Great Spirit dwells.'

"'And so, we shall call this land our own and live here, from this day forever.'

"It was in this way," Gray Eagle concluded his story to his two young sons, "that our ancestors first entered this valley in the long ago, led there by their hunting wolves at a time when ice covered much of the earth. We have remained here ever since, living along the Mahikanittuc River, facing our camps toward the sacred cliffs where the Great Spirit has dwelt since the beginning of time."

At the end of his dream, Lone Wolf once again saw the ancient cliffs of the Mahikanittuc, and a lone eagle soaring above.

***

The rays of the morning sun filtered through the seams of the tepee onto Lone Wolf's face, waking him from his sleep. The Great Spirit, Lone Wolf thought, had already risen from his stone lodge in the East and was crossing the earth toward the land of the Blackfoot.

The cool morning air carried with it the fragrance of the tall pines that surrounded the camp. Bird Rattler was already in the medicine lodge, sharing breakfast with a few of the elders, when Lone Wolf entered. They stood up immediately, their faces in shock.

Lone Wolf was dressed as when Bird Rattler had first seen him ride into the land of the Blackfoot. He wore a roach headdress of deer hair, lined with wolf fur, to which a single feather was attached. The full-

42

feathered war bonnet he had worn as Warrior Chief of the Blackfoot was now draped over his arm.

"I have dreamt throughout the night," Lone Wolf addressed them in a subdued voice. "I have seen yet another vision, of a lone eagle soaring above the cliffs that lie far to the East, in the land of my ancestors. It is there that the Great Spirit dwells, and there that I must seek Him out."

Sadness covered Bird Rattler's face. He knew his worst fear was about to come true.

"Perhaps the time is not right, Lone Wolf," Bird Rattler said. "Could this not wait until after the next snow? Your journey will be easier then."

"I can wait no longer," Lone Wolf answered. "The Great Spirit would not appear to me here on our sacred mountain. He sends an omen instead, a lone eagle who once again beckons me to return to the land of my birth. There the Father of all spirits can answer the question that has long burdened my heart. So I must return now, before I no longer have the strength for such a long journey."

Bird Rattler's eyes began to mist. The elders shook their heads in disbelief.

"This very morning," Bird Rattler said, "your destiny was finally revealed to me, in a sign. I saw a salmon, leaping again and again above the rocks as it returned to the stream from which it first drew life. So, too, will you now be like the salmon. But I pray, not sharing its fate."

"And like the salmon," Lone Wolf said, "my soul still struggles with those who have obstructed its rightful course—the white man, and my own brother."

Lone Wolf walked over to Bird Rattler. He handed Bird Rattler the breast beads given to him by Chief Red Hawk long ago, the symbol that he had become a Blackfoot. Then he handed him the feathered headdress of Warrior Chief, which Bird Rattler himself had bestowed on Lone Wolf at the time of Red Hawk's death.

43

Bird Rattler glanced down at the war bonnet he last held over thirty snows before. He wondered if Lone Wolf would ever return to the Blackfoot after his journey to the East. But he was afraid to ask.

The dying flames of the fire cast shadows over the wrinkled face of the old Medicine Man. Lone Wolf embraced his close friend and whispered into his ear, "I will miss you most, Bird Rattler." Then he turned toward the elders.

"You have been my adopted people," Lone Wolf addressed them. "I have lived here among you for many snows, longer than with my people of the East. At the time I lost my own tribe, long since scattered, you gave me a new life. For this I will always be grateful."

Lone Wolf walked slowly out of the lodge, followed by Bird Rattler and the elders. His brown and white pinto, Wacanga, was standing nearby, loaded with a traveling pack. Many of the tribe gathered around as word spread quickly throughout the camp.

After mounting up, Lone Wolf rode into their midst to bid them farewell. "The time has come, my people. I must return to the East, to the place I first knew as a child."

"Remember above all," Lone Wolf continued, abruptly changing his tone, "as I have always warned, keep the white man out of the Northern Plains. Guard jealously this land, and hand it down to your children, as your ancestors have done since the long ago. Sign no treaties with the white man, and be ever wary of his treachery. Only in this way will you remain free to wander the mountains and plains of your birth."

Lone Wolf raised his arm in farewell, and spoke his final words to the Blackfoot people:

"From this day, forever, I will hunt the buffalo no more."

Now they knew for certain that Lone Wolf would never return. Sadness and quiet fell over the camp.

A tear flowed down Bird Rattler's face.

Lone Wolf slowly rode out of camp, following the path that ran along Cut Bank Creek, the same route as when he had entered these lands as a young man.

The people stood at the edge of camp. Bird Rattler went off by himself. They all watched in silence as their beloved Chief steadily made his way into the distance, his figure becoming ever smaller until fading into the horizon out of which he had first appeared.

Through the mountain pass, then into the Northern Plains, Lone Wolf began his travels. Far beyond were the Eastern Woodlands of his birth. A difficult journey lay ahead, one filled with great peril. Lone Wolf knew that many challenges awaited him along the way—including the hated white man.

Chapter 6

Journey East

An eagle flies overhead, its shadow sweeping over the plains below. A man on horseback follows.

***

Looking back one last time, Lone Wolf caught a glimpse of Going-to-the-Sun Mountain. He recalled his vision quest there, and the ominous words spoken by Bird Rattler alongside Swift Elk's grave:

"The white man now rules the Eastern Woodlands of your birth. Would you not put your freedom, your life, in great peril were you to return?"

But Lone Wolf was determined. He would return! And like the salmon in Bird Rattler's own vision, he would overcome whatever obstacles might lie ahead, or die along the way.

Lone Wolf kept riding until the mountains were no longer in sight. Treeless plains now stretched all around him. He felt a sense of awe from the vastness of the land and sky that seemed to go on forever.

His horse veered off toward a clump of grass. Lone Wolf dismounted to allow him to feed. They had been companions of the trail for nearly twenty snows. He called his brown and white pinto, "Wacanga," for the sweet grass he always seemed to find. Of all the horses he had ridden, Wacanga was Lone Wolf's favorite, a loyal animal whose own scars bore testimony to its unfaltering courage in the battles the two had shared.

Lone Wolf remounted, then made his way toward a nearby spring.

A cloud of dust rose not far from the water hole. Must be buffalo, he thought.

Stretching high above his horse, Lone Wolf strained to make out the small figures in the distance. His heart began to race as he caught sight of mounted warriors—Kutenai.

He was far outnumbered. Should he retreat back through Cut Bank Pass? There the Blackfoot could easily come out to his rescue and make short work of them. But he would rather be killed than lose face in this way.

Up ahead was a dry stream bed. He made a break across the open plains, trying to take cover before being seen. Once down within the ravine, he pulled up against the earthen embankment.

He heard approaching hoofbeats overhead. They were in a gallop. But were they coming after him or just passing by? He waited anxiously. The hoofbeats grew louder. Then they appeared above, lined along the rim of the ravine—Kutenai on horseback, with outstretched spears pointed down. They had seen him take cover.

Lone Wolf quickly turned his horse around, retreating to the opposite side. They were there too, blocking his escape.

The Kutenai leader motioned to Lone Wolf to ride up out of the ravine and approach him. Other warriors immediately rode down from the opposite side. Lone Wolf was surrounded, with spears pointed at him from all sides, some draped with scalps.

The Kutenai looked at him curiously. Lone Wolf raised his arm in greeting. There was no response.

"Of what tribe are you?" asked the leader, whose face was covered with bands of red and black war paint. "I do not recognize your strange manner of dress."

"I am clothed as a Weckquasgeek," Lone Wolf answered, "a tribe of the Eastern Woodlands."

"Why do you roam so far?"

47

"I am returning, after many snows, to the land of my birth, to seek out the Great Spirit who dwells there."

The Kutenai leader motioned with his arm for his warriors to put down their spears. It seemed this ordeal would be over quickly, Lone Wolf thought, and he could continue on his way.

"Wait!" called out one of the warriors, who had been the farthest from their captive. He galloped up to Lone Wolf. Taking a closer look at the battle scars across his chest, he asked his name.

"I am Lone Wolf."

No sooner had they heard his name than the warriors immediately raised their spears, pointing them once again at their encircled captive.

His name had long been known throughout the Northern Plains: Lone Wolf, Warrior Chief of the Blackfoot-Blood. They had done battle many times before, with Lone Wolf always the victor.

"Do you know who I am?" the warrior demanded.

"No, I have never seen you before."

"But you saw my father before."

"How so?" Lone Wolf asked.

"Long past, when you came upon a Kutenai hunting party that had captured your Chief, you killed my father with your spear. The lone survivor of that massacre recounted the story to me. I was only a child then, and was never to know my father, because of you."

The Kutenai raised his spear and pointed it at Lone Wolf.

"Wait!" Lone Wolf shouted, causing the encircling horses to bolt backwards. "Your father was killed as we fought each other, during the rescue of my Chief. Would you not have done the same had you been in my place?"

The Kutenai said nothing. He lifted his spear once again.

"You seek revenge for your father, slain in battle," Lone Wolf said, now addressing the leader rather than the challenger. "Then I, in turn, claim the right as a warrior to defend myself in battle."

The leader nodded his head in agreement. A startled look came over the face of the challenger. Lone Wolf knew the Kutenai leader must respect such a request, or otherwise dishonor the warrior code.

When the signal was given, both Lone Wolf and the challenger dismounted. They squared off immediately, each with a stone knife held outstretched.

The Kutenai slashed wildly at Lone Wolf. Lone Wolf stepped back out of reach, and waited.

The Kutenai then charged ahead, throwing all his weight into the attack.

Lone Wolf lunged forward, driving his knee into the chest of the Kutenai. The Kutenai fell to the ground, gasping for breath.

The leader, watching all from the vantage of his horse, started to laugh, then caught himself.

Lone Wolf, seeing the adversary beginning to recover his senses, jumped on him. He placed a stone knife tightly against his throat.

The encircling Kutenai looked on, expecting a quick kill, Lone Wolf's right as a warrior defending himself.

"I have no wish to take your life," Lone Wolf said to his helpless challenger. "I killed your father not out of hatred or revenge, but out of duty as a warrior to rescue my Chief. If you are a true warrior, you will understand."

Lone Wolf stood up, towering over his victim who still lay on the ground. He walked toward the leader, to address him:

"As I said, I am called 'Lone Wolf.' I was once the Warrior Chief of the Blackfoot, but I am that no more, as time and fate have conspired against me. I return to the land of my ancestors. I return as a Weckquasgeek of the Eastern Woodlands, a people who have never called you enemy nor waged war against you. In their name I ask for passage through your lands."

Lone Wolf sensed a hesitation on the part of the leader. The hatred between the Kutenai and Blackfoot ran deep. But to take him prisoner, now, made no sense.

He noticed the Kutenai leader's breast beads. In the center was an ornament made of carved bone, depicting a wolf's head.

"I am of the Wolf Clan, as are you." Lone Wolf said, pointing to the strip of wolf's fur lining his headroach. "I ask for passage as one of your Clan."

The Kutenai leader, without further hesitation, signaled to his warriors to put down their spears.

"You are of our own Wolf Clan, so you may pass as a Weckquasgeek returning to your homeland," the leader said.

An opening was made in the circle of warriors, allowing Lone Wolf to retrieve his horse. After mounting up, he approached the Kutenai and addressed them:

"The people of the plains have long fought each other. The time has come for all the great tribes to join together—Kutenai, Blackfoot, Cheyenne and Sioux. They must unite and fight the white man instead. If the tribes of the plains do not stand as one, then not even the fierce Blackfoot can keep the white man from taking these lands, and your freedom as well. Heed my words, Kutenai Warriors, keep the white man from ever entering your lands!"

The Kutenai leader answered. "The words you speak are wise, Lone Wolf, great Warrior Chief of The Blackfoot. My heart is now sad that all our tribes could not have united long before, when a chief such as yourself could have led us. But I will, nonetheless, remember your words."

"Go in peace, Lone Wolf," the leader said, raising his arm in farewell. "May you safely reach the land of your ancestors and there rejoin your own people."

Lone Wolf raised his arm, in turn, then rode off. They were soon out of sight.

How strange life was, Lone Wolf thought as he made his way across the plains, that the Kutenai, long enemies of the Blackfoot, should be the last to bid him farewell.

The Kutenai's words now came back to mind: "May you safely reach the land of your ancestors and there rejoin your own people."

But to what was he returning, Lone Wolf asked himself? Had not all his people been driven out, at the time of the forced march? And what about his brother, Rising Bear? Was it possible he had managed to remain behind, and was still alive?

He would never know, nor of that other matter which had long burdened his heart, until he reached the Eastern Woodlands of his birth. First, though, a difficult journey awaited him, one that would put his life in great peril, as Bird Rattler had warned. He dared not imagine what new dangers now lay ahead.

Chapter 7

Winter of Despair

Lone Wolf continued on his journey, riding southeast into the lands of the Cheyenne, long enemies of the Blackfoot. Reaching the Yellowstone River, he waited until dark before crossing. As he swam alongside his horse in the bitter cold waters, he held on tightly to avoid being swept downstream.

Ahead lay the Big Horn Mountains. Traveling over these uninhabited peaks would save him a great distance, he realized, and avoid the danger of being taken captive. Lone Wolf was determined—like the salmon, he would overcome any obstacle in his way. But another danger now awaited him, having disregarded Bird Rattler's warning to delay his journey until spring.

As he rode into the foothills, snow had already begun to fall. In the distance, he saw a grizzly bear heading to its winter den. He knew the snow would become deeper, for the grizzly always waited for the first heavy snowfall, so that both its tracks and scent would be covered after entering its den.

Lone Wolf made his way up toward Cloud Peak, the highest mountain in the Big Horn Range. The temperature began to drop rapidly. As his hands grew numb, he held them tightly against his horse. The animal warmed them quickly.

He stopped to unpack a bearskin coat, with hood. Thick fur lined the inside, while the outer surface of hide had been treated with bear fat to repel water. He put on buckskin leggings, then remounted and continued on his way.

The snow became deeper as Lone Wolf rode higher toward Cloud Peak. Flakes began to cling to his clothing and to the winter fur of his horse. He steadily made his way toward the mountain summit, through an area where there were few trees, each standing alone in an expanse of white. Beyond was a pass between an adjoining peak, leading down to the opposite side. As he crossed into the upper range, the wind blew more fiercely. The bitter cold now made him feel light-headed.

Suddenly, Lone Wolf pulled up on the reins of his horse. He strained to bring his eyes into sharper focus.

There in the distance was a man on horseback, riding down from the snow-covered crags. How could there be any living person in these heights, and in this bitter cold?

The mounted figure raced across the slope toward Lone Wolf. A cloud of whirling snow surrounded both rider and horse, as though enveloped within a blizzard that seemed to follow them at every turn. The howling wind that accompanied them grew louder.

Lone Wolf pulled out his spear.

The strange figure closed in swiftly, then stopped abruptly in front of him. Lone Wolf's horse reared up.

Was he imagining this, Lone Wolf thought, or had the cold affected his mind?

The specter waved his hand above his head. The blizzard that surrounded him and his mount quickly subsided. He appeared to be an old man, with long white hair and beard from which icicles hung. His exposed face was pale and lifeless. In each pupil of his eyes could be seen whirling specks, as though a miniature blizzard raged within. He wore a coat of fur, covered with snow. In his hand was a spear, held upright, made from a sliver of jagged ice.

The horse, like its rider, was covered with snow and icicles that hung from its winter fur. Its mane and tail nearly reached the ground. Mist streamed from both nostrils in powerful blasts.

Lone Wolf quickly put away his spear. He tried to speak, but his voice failed him.

"Why do you cross my domain?" the specter asked. Billows of snow spewed from his mouth as he spoke. "This highest of mountains I claim as my own. No mortal is permitted to enter here, not even to pass."

"But who, or what are you?" Lone Wolf finally said.

"Who am I? What am I?" the specter laughed. "Do you not recognize me, after all the years that I have swept over your lands? I am the Spirit of the Snows."

"Of what snows?" Lone Wolf asked.

"You fool of a mortal! I am the Spirit of all snows that have ever fallen, or will ever fall. Such snows are of me, and I of them. Do you not recognize me now, Lone Wolf? I am the Spirit of the Snows of whom you were first taught as a child."

"You must truly be a spirit," Lone Wolf acknowledged, "for you knew my name before I spoke it."

"No mortal need tell me his name. I have known you and your people from the time I blew the first blizzard over your ancestral lands. And I have returned to visit you ever since, even among your adopted tribe."

"Indeed you have," Lone Wolf said. "Your visits have been of such regularity that we measure the passage of time by them."

"This I know. You can tell me nothing at all, mortal, that I do not already know, but one thing."

"Yes, Spirit?" Lone Wolf said, surprised that a spirit of nature would not know everything.

"Why do you pass through my domain?" the Spirit asked again.

"I am returning to the land of my birth, far in the Eastern Woodlands," Lone Wolf answered.

"These lands I know well, since I first covered them with the great ice in the long ago," the Spirit said. "But notwithstanding, you may not pass this way. You must travel around these mountains I claim as my own.

"Now be gone with you," the Spirit said, just as Lone Wolf was about to speak. "Be gone, mortal, or with one blast of my breath I shall turn you and your mount into pillars of ice, for all eternity!"

With that warning, the Spirit of the Snows turned his horse around, preparing to ride off.

"Wait!" Lone Wolf shouted, startling the Spirit's horse. "Like the salmon returning to the waters of its birth, I do not have time to travel around obstacles that lie in my way."

"So obstinate!" the Spirit replied as a blast of snow billowed out of his mouth, forcing Lone Wolf and his horse backwards. "How dare you, a mere mortal, challenge me in my own domain!"

"I shall pass this way," Lone Wolf said, "for I am a Warrior Chief and have wandered freely throughout my life. No man, nor spirit of nature has ever stopped me."

"You are no longer a Warrior Chief, Lone Wolf, since you left the Blackfoot. Nor were you ever the Warrior Chief of your own people, the Weckquasgeek."

These words found their mark in Lone Wolf's heart, inflicting more pain than any snow or bitter cold ever could.

"I warn you once again!" the Spirit said. "Do not pass this way or I shall make you feel pain and suffering as you have never known before."

"What could you ever know of pain and suffering felt within the heart of a mortal, you who are but a cold, lifeless spirit? You know nothing of a mortal's sufferings that plague him in his earthly life, like the pain felt by a father at the death of his son."

"Be silent, mortal, for such matters do not concern me," the Spirit said, becoming more annoyed.

"I have long been a warrior," Lone Wolf continued. "Pain has been my constant companion, never deterring me from my course."

"I warn you one last time, Lone Wolf. Do not pass this way, or you will feel my twin arrows of snow and cold as never before, and your journey will end here within these mountains."

"I shall pass this way," Lone Wolf said, "for I so will it, and no spirit may ever interfere with the free will of a mortal."

"Since you remain obstinate," the Spirit answered, "I will not stop you now. But you will have to overcome all my fury to pass through these lands. Then we shall see what kind of warrior you truly are."

"So be it," Lone Wolf said.

The Spirit of the Snows quickly turned his horse around and rode back up the mountain. The whirling blizzard that had enveloped him earlier suddenly reappeared. Lone Wolf watched him return to his winter den high within the ice-covered crags. As the mounted figure faded from sight, the snow fell heavier.

Had this been a dream, Lone Wolf thought, or had the cold affected his mind? No matter, he would not be deterred from his journey to the East - not by any mortal, nor by any spirit.

***

Lone Wolf continued on his way, riding through the snow toward the upper mountain pass. The snow fell heavier still. Soon it turned into a blizzard.

The wind-driven flakes covered Lone Wolf in white, sticking to his clothing and the winter fur of his horse. They now resembled the Spirit who had unleashed all his fury against them.

The snow grew deeper, nearly reaching the underbelly of his horse. The animal trudged through the drifts, struggling to lift each leg.

As the snow blew steadily into their faces, they soon became blinded. The wind whistled through the needles of the last remaining pine and spruce trees. Then Lone Wolf heard a sound, which he had known since a child, the low, muffled howl distinctive to the dense needles of a spruce.

They plodded ever slower through the deepening snow, the bitter cold numbing all their senses. The blizzard continued to rage. They would perish for certain, Lone Wolf feared. The Spirit's threatening words returned to mind, "I shall turn you and your mount into pillars of ice."

"Help me, Great Spirit," Lone Wolf cried out in despair. "Help me survive this ordeal."

There was no answer, only the wind.

Then he heard, again, the low, muffled howl. Changing his course, he headed toward its source, still blinded by snow.

When he could go no farther, Lone Wolf saw the faint shadow of a tree directly ahead. Its fragrance confirmed it was a spruce. The tall tree stood like a last, lone sentinel on the snow-covered wasteland. The wind had given up its secret.

Lone Wolf dismounted and sank into the snow, up to his waist. He struggled to move, summoning all his remaining strength. Leaning his weight forward, he plowed through the snow toward the giant old tree. His horse followed. There was no time to waste, or for certain they would both freeze to death.

The lower branches of the spruce, weighted with snow, were bent to the ground. The spaces between were filled with drifts.

Lone Wolf unpacked a stone ax. He noticed an indentation between two lower limbs. Immediately he began chopping off branches between the dense limbs, working his way toward the center of the tree. As branches fell, an opening just wide enough to enter took form. Near the trunk, he hewed out a cavern-like space. The wind-driven snow continued its assault as Lone Wolf worked feverishly to escape its deadly reach.

Just when it seemed he would drop from exhaustion, all was finished. Lone Wolf pulled on the reins of his horse, but the frightened animal refused to enter the narrow opening. He pulled harder still, until

57

Wacanga was fully within the cavern that lay beneath the snow-laden limbs.

Picking up cut branches, Lone Wolf pushed them back into the passage opening, sealing it off. He packed the branches with snow, leaving no space through which the wind could reach into their shelter. The howl of the wind became muffled. Lone Wolf and his horse were now enclosed beneath the spruce, the last remaining tree in an expanse of white.

To avoid the sharp needles of surrounding branches, Lone Wolf forced his pinto to lie down. The ground within the shelter, protected from snow by overhanging limbs, was covered with a thick layer of yellow needles. Within their winter den, it was dry and comfortable.

They were both famished. Lone Wolf unpacked dried berries that he had taken with him for his journey. Holding a large quantity of the sweet fruit in both hands, he mixed it with melted snow and fed it to his horse. The pinto nearly snapped off Lone Wolf's fingers as it ate, then licked the tangy juices off his hands with its long, raspy tongue.

The smoked buffalo meat, which he had also packed for his journey, Lone Wolf devoured like a famished grizzly.

Outside their shelter-within-the-tree, the wind blew furiously, causing the upper limbs to sway. As the blizzard raged, drifting snow collected on the surrounding branches, providing greater protection for the two mortal creatures huddled within.

Once they had both eaten, exhaustion from their ordeal set in. The dried needles covering the ground of their shelter made for soft, fragrant bedding.

Lone Wolf lay down, wrapped in his bearskin coat. He rolled close to his horse, to share their body warmth. They were now safe, beneath the snow-laden limbs of the old spruce.

The two exhausted creatures fell into deep sleep, while the blizzard continued to rage outside their winter den. Like the wise old grizzly, they too would sleep through the Spirit's fury.

***

There, in a dream, Lone Wolf saw snow, from an earlier time, a wind-blown snow falling on a long procession of men, women and children, treading their way between mounted soldiers. They were his people, the Weckquasgeek, being driven from their lands in the East by Dutch and English settlers. Following a surprise attack on their village, they were to be resettled to the white man's reservation far to the west, on lands that had once belonged to the Oklahoma.

In that long line was Lone Wolf, as a young man, walking alongside his elderly mother.

The people were all on foot. Forced to surrender their furs, they had been given cloth blankets to wrap around themselves. The mounted soldiers were dressed in winter uniforms.

The men of the tribe were at the head of the long line, their bows and spears having been taken away. The young children had been crying at first, but now they, too, walked silently. A woman carried an infant in a cradleboard on her back. The infant no longer made any sound.

There was little time for rest. The people were driven onward throughout the day. Lone Wolf's mother had become weakened from the forced march. She had contracted the white man's pox disease shortly before and seemed to be recovering until this ordeal sapped her strength.

"Can my mother ride one of the pack horses?" Lone Wolf asked the leader of the mounted soldiers, called 'Sergeant Cody' by the other whites. "She is weak and hardly able to walk."

59

"Have any furs left to trade, Injun?" Cody said from the vantage of his saddle.

"None. Your men have taken everything from us, before our journey began."

"Well then, she has to walk. Wouldn't want to overload the pack horses, anyway, since they got full loads from the furs you people gave us." He laughed.

They trudged their way through the steadily-falling snow. As the day wore on, the people walked slower. The mounted soldiers kept pushing them harder to maintain their pace.

Past midday, they stopped to eat. The food supplies had run low. The people were given a watery soup made from melted snow and dried beans. A squirrel, fur and all, had been thrown into the boiling kettle. The soldiers had their own rations.

As soon as they had eaten, the march resumed. Lone Wolf's mother grew weaker and had difficulty keeping up.

Lone Wolf asked the Sergeant again if she could ride one of the packhorses. And once again, the Sergeant refused.

Putting his arm under his mother's shoulder, Lone Wolf helped her keep up with the others.

"I can manage on my own," she said. "Save your strength for yourself, Lone Wolf. I am old and have already lived my life. It is more important that you continue on, with yours. There are many things that yet await you."

What life? Lone Wolf thought. To be herded like animals, and driven to a strange land as captives.

The group stopped that evening and made camp, sleeping in small tents. His mother's forehead now burned with fever. When she went to sleep that night, Lone Wolf added his blanket to hers to protect her from the wind that blew in through the seams of the tent.

In the morning he turned to wake her. Her body was cold. She had died in her sleep. The gentle smile that Lone Wolf had known since he was a child, was still on her face. His eyes filled with tears, and his heart with hatred.

He went out to search for Sergeant Cody to tell him what had happened.

"So what do you want me to do about it now?" the Sergeant said, looking down from his horse.

Lone Wolf motioned to him for a tool to dig with, the word for which he did not know—the white man's metal tool that could cut through the ground to make a grave.

"We don't have time to bury anyone, and we don't have shovels," Sergeant Cody answered. "We're breaking camp right now and leavin' in ten minutes. Put her over there in that snow drift."

Lone Wolf seethed with hatred as he looked up into Cody's hardened face.

He carried his mother's body to beneath a nearby tree. Using a pointed stick broken from a limb, he tried to dig a grave in the frozen ground. The stick snapped in two.

Lone Wolf struggled to bury his mother deep within a nearby snowdrift. He knew that it was only a matter of time before scavenging predators would find her body and devour what was left of her.

After reciting prayers of burial, Lone Wolf spoke his parting words.

"Forgive me, Mother, for burying you this way. I will join you one day in the Spirit Land, after my own life is done. There our family will again be together, as the proud people we once were."

Hatred swelled in Lone Wolf's heart as he walked back to rejoin his people. They had watched from a distance.

The forced march continued. The following day, they stopped to make camp for the evening. A soldier reached into a bundle on the back of a packhorse, searching for rations. Two metal shovels fell to the

61

ground, striking each other. Lone Wolf, a short distance away, heard the sound and turned to look. Sergeant Cody, who saw what had happened, quickly rode off.

Lone Wolf would never forget.

***

As Lone Wolf and his horse lay safe within their winter den beneath the old spruce, he continued to dream:

Again, he saw his people, those who had survived, at the end of their forced march. They were entering the gates of a timber stockade. The 'fort', as the white man called it, was at the center of the reservation.

After all were inside, Sergeant Cody had the packhorses brought over to the storeroom.

"Get these Injuns to unload," Cody ordered one of his corporals. "Now that we're two days late, I've got to report to the Colonel and make excuses for myself. This is gonna mess up my chances of a promotion, because of these lazy savages. And keep a close eye on that one over there called 'Lone Wolf,' he's going to be trouble."

The people began unloading bundles from the packhorses. The older members of the tribe, many near exhaustion, sat on the wooden floor of a nearby porch. They wrapped themselves in their blankets and watched the others, not knowing what was to happen to them. There was fear in their eyes, and a deep sadness.

Lone Wolf already knew what awaited them. He had heard stories of similar places. It was here at such reservations, he had been told, that the Indians were kept confined to a small area of land, no longer free to roam the forests and mountains.

He looked again, to where the old people were seated on the porch. He felt sorrow for them and for his tribe, what was left of it. Nearly half his people had been killed in the surprise attack on their village, and half again of those remaining had died along the forced

62

march through the snow. Those who managed to survive both ordeals were now to become captives of the white man. Never before had his tribe known such a winter of despair.

He would rather be dead, Lone Wolf thought, than to lose the freedom he had always cherished. Surveying the initial confusion of their arrival, he realized his best chance was to make a quick break, when least expected. His father's words from long ago returned to mind, "Never allow your enemy any advantage—always strike quickly!"

Now was the time. Sergeant Cody had disappeared into the storeroom to supervise the storage of furs, worried that some of his soldiers might steal the furs he had taken for himself. Lone Wolf walked over to one of the pack horses, a black stallion that had caught his eye. He helped the others in unloading the bundles from the stout animal. Once it was free of its burden, he jumped onto the back of the startled horse and kicked it repeatedly into a gallop. They charged through the gates of the fort, which one of the soldiers had left open. The horse soldiers watched in shock, while his own people cheered him on.

Sergeant Cody was summoned from the storeroom. He broke into a rage, threatening to court martial the corporal in charge of watching the gates. After he had calmed down, Cody ordered his men to mount up for a chase party. The horses were retrieved from the corral and re-saddled, but valuable time had been lost.

When they had finally ridden out through the gates and into the woods that surrounded the fort, Lone Wolf was well out of sight. The search party broke up into two patrols and combed the area for his tracks. Once they picked up his trail, they reassembled and pursued him until dark, with Sergeant Cody at the lead.

Lone Wolf, in fear of being captured, never stopped for rest, driving his stallion relentlessly into the depths of the forest. His eye for good horses had proven true. The sturdy mount did not fail him. He would ride the animal into the ground if he had to, but he would never be taken captive.

The horse soldiers, pushed on by Sergeant Cody, pursued Lone Wolf for days. Once within the mountains, Lone Wolf knew there was no man alive that could ever track him down. He was free, once again.

Heading northwest toward the upper Missouri, Lone Wolf rode deep into lands the white man had not yet entered. The surrounding landscape seemed to lure him on, ever farther, to a destiny yet unknown.

Finally, he made his way into the Northern Plains. There he found a people of great hunters and warriors whom one day he would lead into battle as their Warrior Chief — the Blackfoot, masters of the Northern Plains.

*　*　*

The sound of the night-long blizzard had grown faint when Lone Wolf awoke from his sleep. He sat quietly within the shelter, recalling his dream of his mother, and of the gentle smile still on her face the morning she died. Perhaps on his journey east, Lone Wolf thought, he should return to the reservation. There he could seek out his people, those who were left — and Sergeant Cody.

He poked a hole with his long spear through the snow-covered limbs and surrounding drifts. The bright rays of the sun pierced the shelter, blinding him momentarily. He dug his way out between the branches, then broke through into daylight. His horse followed.

The snow and wind had now stopped. All was still.

But where was the Spirit of the Snows, Lone Wolf wondered? Perhaps it had all been a dream. Or was the Spirit asleep within his own winter den?

Lone Wolf would not linger and give the Spirit another chance to strike. He mounted his horse and made his way across the deep snow, up toward the adjoining peaks, then finally through the pass that led over to the eastern slopes of the Big Horn Mountains.

On the far side of the pass, sheltered by the summit, the snow was not as deep. Travel was easier as Lone Wolf headed downward. He rode until he was on the lower mountain range, well out of reach of the Spirit of the Snows.

Lone Wolf realized that once again, as throughout his life, he had been put to the test. He had survived the Spirit's fury of snow and cold. And once again, as he remembered the death of his mother, the hatred he had long carried for the white man returned, more bitter than ever.

The snow was nearly gone as Lone Wolf rode out of the foothills of the Big Horn Mountains. He patted his horse, Wacanga, and continued on his journey.

The surrounding country now looked familiar. He had passed this way long before, when fleeing the white man's fort where his people had been taken captive. But how many, he wondered, had survived?

And whatever became of Sergeant Cody?

Chapter 8

A Captive People

The Big Horn Mountains were now far behind as Lone Wolf rode his horse along the Platte River. He followed it as it flowed southeast, into the lands of the Nebraska, a tribe that had long since vanished.

What of his own people, he wondered? What had become of the few that had survived the forced march to the white man's reservation? Should he travel out of his way to see them one last time? Perhaps they would have word of his brother, who had disappeared at the time their village was attacked. Then there was Sergeant Cody, whose cruelty Lone Wolf had never forgotten.

But thirty snows had fallen since Lone Wolf had fled the reservation. Few if any of his people would still be alive, he thought. And as for Sergeant Cody, by this time he must have been replaced by a younger soldier.

Lone Wolf turned his horse and headed due East, back to his original course. Suddenly he heard the piercing cry of a bird. He looked up and saw a white-headed eagle circling overhead. The eagle flew off to the southeast, toward the reservation. Once again, an omen! He must follow, instead, to whatever destiny awaited him there.

For nearly one moon Lone Wolf rode through the lands once belonging to the Kansa and the Oklahoma tribes, retracing the route he had taken after fleeing the fort. He finally reached the Washita River. Recalling that the reservation lay on the opposite side, he waited until dark before crossing.

The following morning Lone Wolf found the forest surrounding the clearing around the fort. It was through this forest that he had first made his escape. Riding to the edge of the trees, he saw in the distance the stockade walls of the fort, standing by itself. There, too, was a patrol of horse soldiers, in their blue uniforms. But where were his people?

Now more cautious than ever, he scouted the surrounding land. By midday he finally spotted an encampment, located in a flat, dry area, a good distance from the fort. There were no horse soldiers in sight.

He rode up to the encampment then slowly made his way through the center. How strange! There were only a few tepees, with the remaining shelters made of scraps of wood pieced together. This could not be the village of his people, he thought, the proud Weckquasgeek of the Eastern Woodlands.

As he continued riding between the shelters, he saw a scattering of men and women outside. Few took much notice of him. At the end of the row he dismounted, in front of a tepee that stood by itself. Nearby, an old man sat on a rotted tree stump.

"Can you tell me, old man, where I might find the Chief of this tribe?"

"Ha! We have no Chief, for there are no warriors left to lead," the old man answered, looking Lone Wolf over carefully.

"And who are you?" the old man asked, "that you wear the clothing and headdress of our people and speak our tongue."

Lone Wolf's heart sank.

"I am Lone Wolf. I was once of your tribe. I fled from this place the day we first arrived, after having been driven here by the white man. I have lived ever since among the Blackfoot of the Northern Plains."

"But to what family did you belong?" the old man asked, now standing to take a better look at the visitor.

"I am the son of Chief Gray Eagle, who was killed by the white man at the last battle in our homeland. Do you remember me: Lone Wolf, son of Chief Gray Eagle?"

"Son of Chief Gray Eagle...Gray Eagle...Lone Wolf? But of course!" the old man cried out. "I remember you now. You were a young warrior at the time. How you fled so quickly from the fort before the horse soldiers knew what had happened. I remember, too, my feelings of regret for not having joined you in your escape.

"And, of course, I remember your father, Chief Gray Eagle. I remember him, indeed, in those happier times back East, where we hunted together. A close friend of mine...close friends...very close friends we were...but my memory fades, and it becomes ever harder to recall."

"Do you remember my brother, Rising Bear?" Lone Wolf asked the old man.

"Rising Bear...Rising Bear...yes, now I remember. You were brothers-of-the-same-birth. So difficult it was to tell the two of you apart."

"Do you know what ever happened to him?"

"No, Lone Wolf. Your brother disappeared at the time of the surprise attack on our village. No one has seen him since."

Was his brother still alive, Lone Wolf wondered. But how could he have survived in the Eastern Woodlands during all that time, amid the white man?

"Do you remember me, Lone Wolf?" the old man asked. "I was once called 'Swims-Like-A-Beaver,' but I have come to be known as 'Never Scouts.'"

"Yes, now I do," Lone Wolf answered. The facial features of the old man appeared familiar, but like his own, age had exacted its toll. "What is the meaning of this name you have taken?"

"I refused to serve as scout for the horse soldiers, Lone Wolf, and so they named me. It is sad to say, but our men, the few that are left, have joined the blue coats as paid scouts. They hunt down other Indians who leave the reservation, and return them to the fort as captives. I could not serve them in this way, and so the horse soldiers have given me this name, in mockery. To displease them further, I have taken it as my own, in pride."

"And so you should be proud, Never Scouts," Lone Wolf said, patting the old man on the shoulder. "You keep your honor as a warrior. But tell me, what has happened here to our people? Why do they live in this way, in such hovels? And why do they no longer dress in the traditional way, except for yourself?"

"Our fate here has been a miserable one, Lone Wolf, from the moment we first set foot in this forsaken place," the old man answered, sitting back down on the rotted tree stump.

"Over time we have become impoverished, both in matters of the world and of the spirit. The land first given to us by the white man's treaty was to be ours for 'as long as the sun shall rise.' This included all the mountains and forest that surround us here," the old man pointed, "stretching beyond to where the Washita River bends to the north. There was enough game for our people to hunt. But soon after, white men intruded into our mountains."

"Did you not complain that these lands had been promised under treaty?" Lone Wolf asked, realizing immediately how foolish his question was.

"We did! Many times! But it was of no use. Just as before with our lands in the East, the white man's word, and his treaties meant nothing. They are easily broken, whenever it suits their needs. Of this, Lone Wolf, I am sure you need no reminding."

"Yes, their treaties, and their word, mean nothing," Lone Wolf said.

"Not long after we settled here," the old man continued, "white men came into our mountains to dig the yellow iron out of the earth. The more they found, the more of their kind followed. Soon the horse soldiers came to take from us all of our mountains and forest. In exchange, they gave us this flat, dry land where we now stand.

"The mountains were no longer ours on which to hunt," the old man went on, now with anger in his voice.

"We were supposed to become herders of sheep, they told us. But they did not understand. Our people are hunters! We have always taken to the hunt, living in the old way. And besides, the ground is so dry that not even a grasshopper can live here very long. Only scrub grass grows in this worthless dirt."

"How, then, do the people live?" Lone Wolf asked.

"The agency brings in food by wagon, from time to time. Our people line up like beggars for these handouts, having lost all their dignity. And the rations, such as flour, are of poor quality, some spoiling before ever reaching us. If we are lucky, though, we may find a snake or gopher to add to our kettles. We have been reduced to paupers, Lone Wolf, no longer able to provide for ourselves and our families, waiting instead for the white man to hand us food and blankets."

Lone Wolf listened in sadness to the old man. He regretted ever having returned. It would have been better to remember his people as they once were—proud hunters of the Eastern Woodlands.

The old man went on with his story.

"With no game to hunt and no way to help ourselves, except as servants of the white man, our warriors began to drink his whiskey, which they gave our scouts as pay. They are now no good to anyone, not even themselves."

"But where are all the rest?" Lone Wolf asked the old man. "Surely there must be more?"

"Those you see, and a few scouts, are all that remain of us," he answered. "They were born here, in captivity. Of our people who originally came from the East, all have died. I alone am left. With my weakening condition, my days, too, are numbered. We lost many, including the young, from the white man's pox disease that spread among us after the march-through-the-snows."

"And so with my own mother," Lone Wolf said. "She died just before our arrival at the fort."

"Yes, Lone Wolf, now that you have refreshed my memory, I do recall that sad time."

"Our numbers are now so few," the old man continued. "They said that soon we will be moved to live amongst another tribe along the Upper Washita River. They say there are no longer enough of us to remain here on our own reservation. We are to live together with other tribes, unknown to us, but whose blood will soon mix with our own. In a short time our people, as we have known them, will be no more."

The old man's eyes were sad again, as he looked down at the ground. He kicked the dust with his frayed moccasin.

"I shall die in a strange place, far from the land of my ancestors," he lamented. "I wish I could return to die in my homeland and rest amongst the sacred graves of our own people."

"I am, myself, returning to the East," Lone Wolf said, "to seek out the Great Spirit, for a matter that has long burdened my heart."

The old man's eyes lit up for a moment. "I wish I could travel with you, Lone Wolf. But as you can see, I am old and decrepit. I have lived for over eighty snows, and no longer able to ride a horse for any distance. I fear I would be a burden, and jeopardize your chances of reaching our ancestral lands. Oh, how my heart aches to join you, on your journey."

Looking down at the old man seated on the tree stump, Lone Wolf again patted him on the shoulder. He, too, wished to take this last survivor of the march-through-the-snows with him on his journey, but the travel was far too difficult and dangerous.

"Farewell, old Weckquasgeek," Lone Wolf said, paying his final respects as he mounted up. "I pray that one day we will meet again in the Spirit Land, and take to the hunt as our people did in the past."

"And so do I, Lone Wolf," the old man said, raising his arm in farewell. "May the Great Spirit watch over you on your journey East."

Lone Wolf rode out of camp, never to look back. He regretted, more than ever, having returned to see his tribe—what was left of it. Some day they would no longer have any collective memory of who they once were, no identity at all as Weckquasgeeks. With the elders gone, and soon the old man himself, there would be no one left to tell them of their legends and of their land back East. And once merged with other tribes and their bloods mixed, they would cease to exist as a people. Then Lone Wolf would be the last of his kind.

**

As he rode off, Lone Wolf felt a sense of relief that he could leave this forsaken place where the remnants of his people lived as captives. How good it was, he reminded himself, to again wander freely through the enchanted forests and mountains that seemed forever to lure him on.

He pushed Wacanga into a gallop and headed back into the foothills, trying to make up for lost time. Once he entered the cover of the surrounding woods, he knew he could breathe easier since he would no longer be exposed on the open prairie.

No sooner had he ridden under the canopy of trees, than he found himself surrounded by horse soldiers. Their rifles were all pointed at him.

"We'd seen you down below," said one of the soldiers, wearing the insignia of an officer. "We've been waiting for you. Now take him prisoner," he ordered. "He looks like a renegade."

"I am not of this land," Lone Wolf explained to the Indian scout riding with the patrol. "I am passing through and wish only to continue along my way."

The scout translated to the officer.

"I don't care who you are. An Indian is an Indian. We're taking you back with us."

The soldiers began talking amongst themselves, of what they planned to do with their share of the bounty for capturing a renegade. They tied Lone Wolf's hands behind his back, while he was still mounted, and took him to the fort.

Lone Wolf was stricken with fear as he approached the gates. This was the fort from which he had escaped over thirty snows before. His people had been confined here after the forced march. Now it would be his turn.

No sooner had the patrol entered the fort than he was taken to the guardhouse. The soldiers threw Lone Wolf into a dark cell, then locked the timber door behind him. The clank of the sliding bolt sent chills up Lone Wolf's spine. He was finally a captive of the white man, like the rest of his people.

Later that day Lone Wolf was taken out of the cell. With his hands still tied behind his back, he was led to the orderly room. The guards shoved him through the doorway toward a large oak desk in the middle of the room. Bent over behind the desk, shuffling through a lower drawer, sat a gray-haired soldier. The seams in the blue jacket of his uniform were stretched apart, ready to snap.

As he lifted up his face, they recognized each other immediately.

"Well, I'll be..." the soldier said. "After all these years, just weeks before I'm ready to retire, I finally caught you!"

Lone Wolf could not believe his eyes. He was still here, Sergeant Cody, the officer in charge of the forced march that had driven his tribe from their lands; the same Sergeant Cody who said there were no packhorses for Lone Wolf's mother to ride, nor any shovel to bury her with.

The Sergeant stood up and walked around the desk. He stared Lone Wolf in the face. His putrid breath made Lone Wolf sick to his stomach.

"Lone Wolf! I remember your name, even after all this time. Do you know why, Lone Wolf, do you know why I remember you so well? Because you're the worthless savage that ruined my military career! I was in line for promotion to a commissioned officer, until I led your miserable tribe to this fort. Then you escaped from my custody. The Colonel held me personally responsible, since I was in charge of the escort. He blamed me for your escape. They wrote it up in my records, and it's been there ever since. If it wasn't for your escape, it would'a been a perfect mission, and I would'a had my bars long ago."

What kind of soldier was this, Lone Wolf thought, recalling once again the suffering his own people had endured under Cody's ruthless command during the march-through-the-snow.

"I would'a been a commissioned officer now, instead of just an N.C.O.," Cody shouted in Lone Wolf's face, pointing to the gold-braided sergeant stripes on his sleeve. "By this time I'd be at least a major. But you had to ruin it all by escaping from the fort. You made me look bad, real bad, and it's cost me ever since."

Sergeant Cody continued shouting into Lone Wolf's face, his breath making Lone Wolf sicker still.

"But now you're gonna pay, Lone Wolf, for what you did to me," Cody ranted, his face flushed red, "After all these years, I finally got the worthless Injun who messed up my military career. When I get through with you, you'll be sorry you ever came back to these parts."

Cody ripped the roach headdress from Lone Wolf's hair and threw it on the floor. He grabbed Lone Wolf, his hands still tied behind him, and pushed him against the wall. "Take this savage away!" he ordered. "And I warn you, if he escapes again I'll personally see to it that you both get court martialed and hung!"

Lone Wolf was taken back to the guardhouse and locked in the cell for the night, under double watch. The soldiers standing guard, in fear of Sergeant Cody's threat, kept Lone Wolf's hands tied behind his back.

Lone Wolf dared not fall asleep. How unbelievable this was, he thought. It was Lone Wolf's people, including women and children, and his sick mother, who had suffered and died. Yet, Cody felt he was the one who had been wronged. A perverted mind such as this could not be trusted, Lone Wolf realized. The longer he waited to make his move, the greater the danger, and the more difficult it would be to escape. His father's words came to mind once again, "Never allow your enemy any advantage — always strike quickly."

He must strike, then, before it was too late, or he would spend the rest of his life as a captive of the white man.

In the darkness of the cell, Lone Wolf could not see at all. He felt around with his hands, still tied behind his back, and found a ledge of stone that protruded from a wall. Careful not to make any sound, he pressed the rope that bound his wrists against the stone ledge, rubbing up and down to cut the fibers. His mind grew wild with fear as to what might happen to him if he failed. He would end up like the old man seated on the rotted tree stump.

Throughout the night Lone Wolf worked feverishly, scraping the rope behind his back against the stone ledge. The rope cut into his wrists, causing them to bleed. By sunrise, he had severed most of the fibers. He was certain, now, that he could snap the remaining fibers, when the time was right to make his break. There would be one chance and one chance only. The next time, he feared, they would bind him in irons.

He heard the footsteps of approaching guards as their boots struck the stone floor. The door of the cell was unbolted. There were now four, in all. They removed him from the cell, keeping his hands tied behind his

75

back. He was taken directly to the orderly room, without breakfast, or a chance to relieve himself. Sergeant Cody was waiting for him.

"Have you slept well, Lone Wolf?" Cody mocked. "Did they serve you breakfast yet?"

Lone Wolf noticed a crazed look come over Cody.

"Before they do, Injun, we have a surprise for you. I gave it a lot of thought last night and tried to come up with something special that would suit you."

From behind his desk Cody reached down and pulled out a heavy iron chain, with a shackle attached to one end.

Lone Wolf's eyes turned to fear.

"We're going to give you this, Lone Wolf, sort of a 'welcome back' gift," Cody said with a vengeful grin. He rattled the chain in his captive's face.

"You see this iron shackle, my old friend? Well that should fit just nice around your ankle. And the chain," Cody continued, "well that's about six feet long. That'll give you plenty of room to move around, after we stake it down at the other end. That's going to be your very own circle for you to roam in, 'cause we know now how much you Injuns love to roam."

Sergeant Cody again shook the chain and shackle in Lone Wolf's face.

"This is the way you're gonna spend the rest of your life, Lone Wolf, working around the fort here, sweeping up, cleaning the manure out of the stable. But this time, whenever we move you, we're gonna keep the chain on you to make sure you don't escape again. Now how do you like that?" He opened the shackle collar.

Rage rushed through Lone Wolf's veins. He struggled with all his strength to pull his bound hands apart. His face strained in pain. The rope cut deeper into his wrists until they bled again.

The last fibers of rope finally snapped. His hands sprang free from around his back.

Sergeant Cody and the guards stood there for a moment in shock.

Before giving his captors any chance to react, Lone Wolf jumped on top of the desk, then pushed Cody to the floor. He leaped through a glass window, onto the covered porch outside the orderly room. The shattering glass blew outward in a burst of sparkling fragments.

His horse was near the entrance to the stable on the opposite side of the fort, where it had been left overnight. The pinto neighed loudly the moment he saw his missing companion.

Lone Wolf ran across the open court, the four guards and Sergeant Cody chasing him. Rifle shots peppered the dusty ground around him.

Leaping onto his horse, Lone Wolf turned and rode back through his startled pursuers. Two of the guards were knocked to the ground. The main gates of the fort had just opened as a supply wagon made its way through.

"Close those gates!" Sergeant Cody shouted from across the way. "Close those gates before that redskin escapes again!"

Lone Wolf charged through the portal as the wagon passed alongside. The harnessed team became startled. Bolting upwards, the horses overturned the wagon, blocking the opening after Lone Wolf had ridden through.

He was now out of the fort and in the clearing that surrounded it. Gun shots from the stockade turrets whistled past his head. Kicking his pinto repeatedly, he fled across the open field.

If he could make it into the woods, Lone Wolf thought, the advantage would be his. There they would have to track him, and speed would be less of a factor.

Lone Wolf and his horse raced across the clearing. The rifle shots grew heavier. He crouched down against Wacanga, to make for a smaller target. At last he reached the edge of the trees, then disappeared into the forest.

Two soldiers, with Sergeant Cody at the lead, finally rode out of the fort. They chased after Lone Wolf, entering the forest where he had last been seen.

For three days the soldiers tracked him relentlessly, riding until sunset. Lone Wolf pushed on without rest. The hatred carried by Sergeant Cody ran deep, Lone Wolf thought, a hatred sustained for over thirty snows. But his own hatred ran deeper still, for this ruthless Sergeant who had shown no mercy toward his people, nor toward his sick mother during the forced march. If given the chance, Lone Wolf would take his revenge.

Straight ahead was a brook that meandered through the forest. Lone Wolf rode his horse into the streambed, making it difficult for them to pick up his tracks.

The horse soldiers were ordered by Cody to ride on both sides of the stream, searching for hoof prints along the banks.

It would be a while now, Lone Wolf thought, before they could catch up to him. This would be a good time, then, to give his horse a rest. He dismounted and let his pinto feed on grass that grew along the stream.

Lone Wolf lay down, then fell asleep from exhaustion. In what seemed only a moment, he was startled by the sound of horses. He jumped to his feet. Sergeant Cody's figure appeared over a ridge.

"There he is! I see him!" Cody shouted to the two soldiers riding alongside.

Grabbing his bow, Lone Wolf let loose an arrow. The arrow struck the closest rider in the chest, dropping him to the ground.

The other soldier broke in panic. Lone Wolf's second arrow glanced off the buttock of the fleeing horse. The soldier struck his head on an overhanging limb and was knocked to the ground, where he lay motionless.

Only Sergeant Cody was left. He quickly took cover.

Lone Wolf crouched beneath the bushes, moving farther away to stay out of range of Cody's rifle.

A shot rang out, ricocheting off a nearby tree. Then another. Splinters of wood struck Lone Wolf in the face.

"I've finally got ya, Lone Wolf! You're as good as dead," Cody shouted as he closed in for the kill.

A third shot passed through Lone Wolf's hair. The long barrelled rifles of the horse soldiers were very accurate, Lone Wolf realized. His luck could not hold out much longer.

Cody was out of bullets. He stopped to reload.

Lone Wolf moved up to where he could see him clearly. No time to waste! Again, his father's words echoed in Lone Wolf's mind, "Strike quickly!"

Lone Wolf reached into his quiver. His arrows were gone. Grabbing his spear, he charged toward his pursuer.

His figure now fully exposed, Lone Wolf knew he would be killed if Cody reloaded in time. At that moment Cody raised his rifle and took aim.

Lone Wolf stopped suddenly, releasing his spear with the full force of his run.

The spear flew between the trees, slashing through the leaves, then pierced Cody's leg. Cody dropped to the ground. His rifle fell in front of him, just out of reach.

"You broke my leg!" Cody cried out. "You broke my leg!"

As Lone Wolf closed in, Cody stretched to grab his rifle. His face grimaced with pain. He could not move.

Lone Wolf cautiously walked over to where Cody lay on the ground.

"Help me get up, Lone Wolf. I promise I'll get you one of these long rifles for yourself. Just help me get on my horse so I can get back to the fort."

79

Lone Wolf did not answer. He grabbed the reins of Cody's horse standing nearby.

"No, not my horse, not my horse," Cody pleaded.

Slapping its flank, Lone Wolf sent the animal into a gallop, deep into the forest. Then he picked up Cody's rifle and, holding it by the end of the barrel, slammed it against a tree. The rifle shattered into pieces.

After cutting a length of vine, Lone Wolf tied Cody's hands behind his back, as had been done to him. Cody sat helplessly on the ground, blood from his leg soaking the leaves.

"Now you are my captive!" Lone Wolf said.

He took the yellow bandanna from around Cody's neck and tied it over his mouth.

"Your voice has finally been silenced. No longer can you speak your lies."

Lone Wolf pulled out his stone knife. Cody flinched, fearing Lone Wolf would take his revenge.

Pressing the knife against the sleeve of Cody's jacket, Lone Wolf cut off the gold-braided sergeant stripes. He held them in Cody's face. "You are no warrior. You are a man without honor, one who abuses women and children placed in his charge."

He spit on the stripes, then threw them to the ground.

Rage flashed in Lone Wolf's eyes as he knelt down in front of Cody.

"'Do you have a pack horse for my sick mother to ride?'" Lone Wolf shouted in Cody's face. "'Do you have a shovel so I can bury her before the animals come to devour her body?'"

Lone Wolf stood up. He took strips of dried buffalo meat from his pack, and scattered them on the ground around his captive. Cody watched, unable to move.

"Soon a grizzly from these woods will come to claim you as well. But unlike my mother, you will still be alive to watch as it tears at your flesh with its claws."

A horse suddenly appeared from beneath the trees. It was Wacanga. Lone Wolf immediately mounted up and rode off. He pushed deeper into the forest, far from the reach of the soldiers at the fort.

Never again, he vowed, would he be taken captive. To no man and to no spirit would he ever surrender his freedom.

Chapter 9

Flames of Hatred

It was now early spring. Lone Wolf turned his horse and headed northeast, back to his original route. As he crossed the flatlands, he watched the rays of the sun break over the horizon, rising from out of his ancestral lands in the East. His yearning to return grew stronger. Was it possible, he wondered again, that his brother was still there, having survived the attack on their village? But Lone Wolf did not care. It was the Great Spirit, alone, whom he sought at the end of his journey, and the words his father had taken to his grave.

Dry grass still covered the flatlands. There had been no rain, and leaf buds had yet to appear. Lone Wolf was out of water. He rode toward a stand of tall pines in the distance. A forest such as this, he knew, would have a brook hidden within. He had to find it soon, for the lack of water had begun to make him feel faint.

Halfway across the flatlands, he caught sight of a mounted figure riding out of the forest. Lone Wolf looked for cover. There was none.

The strange figure closed in swiftly. Both rider and horse appeared to be enveloped in a cloud of dust. As they drew closer, Lone Wolf stared in disbelief.

The mounted specter was surrounded by swirling smoke. The fur he wore over his shoulders and back was covered with glowing embers.

The smoldering figure of man and horse pulled up abruptly. Lone Wolf's pinto bucked, sending him into the air. When he had quieted the animal down, Lone Wolf took a closer look. He felt heat radiating from the bodies of both rider and horse.

The specter had long hair sticking out of his head in all directions. The red and yellow streaks were not feathers, as they first appeared, but his own hair, within which smoldering pockets flared up sporadically.

Grasped tightly within his hand and held upright was his spear, a lightning bolt of silver-blue flashes, hissing and snapping.

The horse, like its rider, was covered in glowing embers within its singed, ashen hair. Its mane and tail nearly reached the ground. Smoke streamed from both nostrils in powerful blasts.

As the specter began to speak, embers billowed out of his mouth. His voice carried with it a crackling, like that of a burning log.

"Why do you cross my domain?" he asked.

Lone Wolf moved his horse backwards so as not to be scorched by the fiery breath. The eyes of the specter turned bright red as he spoke again.

"This ancient forest of tall pines I claim as my own. No mortal is permitted to enter here, not even to pass."

"But what manner of creature are you?" Lone Wolf asked, choking from the specter's smoky breath. "You are clothed in glowing embers and yet not consumed by them!"

"What manner of creature am I, you ask? What manner of insolence is this that a mortal should question a spirit, and in his own domain at that?"

"A spirit?"

"Yes, a spirit! Do you not recognize a spirit when you see one? I am the Spirit of Fire."

"Of what fire?" Lone Wolf asked.

"You fool of a mortal! I am the Spirit of all fires that have ever burned, or will ever burn. Such fires are of me and I of them. Do you not recognize me now, Lone Wolf? I am the Spirit of Fire of whom you were first taught as a child."

"You must truly be a spirit," Lone Wolf acknowledged, "for you knew my name before I spoke it."

"No mortal need tell me his name. I have known you since you were a child, and my flames burned in the first campfire that ever gave you warmth. My flames have burned in the campfires of your people since the beginning of time."

"Indeed they have," Lone Wolf answered the Spirit, whose powers he knew only too well. "Your fires have been of great benefit to my people. We have cooked and smoked our food with your gift, and we have taken warmth from it during many winters. Without your help, Spirit, we would never have survived the cold we have endured since the long ago when our ancestors once hunted the woolly mammoth."

"This I know, Lone Wolf. I have known your people since I was first sent to them from the ever-burning sun by the Great Spirit himself. There is nothing at all that I do not already know, but one thing."

"Yes, Spirit?" Lone Wolf said, knowing the question that would follow.

"Why do you pass through my domain?" the Spirit asked again.

"I return to the land of my birth, far in the Eastern Woodlands," Lone Wolf answered.

"These lands of the East I know well," the Spirit said. "There the trees are harder to burn, than here in this stand of tall pines. But notwithstanding, you may not pass this way at all. You must travel around this forest I claim as ..."

"I have wandered freely throughout my life," Lone Wolf interrupted.

"Be gone with you, you insolent mortal, or with one blast of my breath I shall burn you and your mount to cinders."

"Wait!" Lone Wolf shouted, startling the Spirit's horse. "Like the salmon returning to the waters of its birth, I do not have time to travel around obstacles that lie in my way."

"So obstinate!" the Spirit said. "I have already spoken. You may not pass this way." Smoke and embers spewed from the Spirit's mouth. Lone Wolf again backed his horse out of range of the scorching breath.

"I warn you for the last time, Lone Wolf. Do not pass this way or I shall make you feel pain and suffering as you have never known before," the Spirit threatened, his fiery breath now coming out of both his mouth and nostrils.

"Like the pain inflicted upon my people when our village was burned to the ground, and our women and children perished in your wanton flames."

"Be silent, Lone Wolf! Was it not foolish mortals like you who misused my gift? Now be gone with you, and rejoin your own kind."

"I shall pass this way," Lone Wolf said, "for I so will it, and no spirit may ever interfere with the free will of a mortal."

"Since you remain obstinate," the Spirit said, "I will not stop you now. But you will have to overcome all my fury to pass through these lands. And then we shall see what kind of warrior you truly are."

"So be it," Lone Wolf answered.

The Spirit of Fire turned his horse around with a jerk of the reins that twisted the animal's neck. He rode back across the flatlands and into the pine forest out of which he had first appeared, leaving behind a wispy trail of smoke.

Had this been a dream, Lone Wolf thought? Or had the lack of water already affected his mind? No matter, he would not be deterred from his journey East, not by any mortal, nor by any spirit.

***

Lone Wolf continued across the flatlands, toward the pine forest ahead where he hoped to find water. He stopped suddenly.

Before reaching the trees, he heard hoofbeats from behind. He turned to look. The Spirit of Fire had reappeared.

Again enveloped in smoke and embers, the Spirit and his horse raced across the flatlands in a frenzy. From his outstretched hand long streaks of flame leaped out of the tip of each finger, setting fire to the tufts of grass below.

Soon everything was ablaze. The wind fanned the flames through the dry grass. Loud crackling could be heard all around as moisture trapped in the straw exploded into steam.

The Spirit turned toward Lone Wolf. "Pass now, you insolent mortal," he laughed. He then disappeared through the thickening smoke that blinded Lone Wolf and irritated his eyes.

The flames swept across the flatlands toward Lone Wolf. He kicked his frightened horse and drove him toward the trees ahead.   Reaching the forest at last, he rode into its depths, well beyond the flames. The sound of flowing water led them to a brook. There Lone Wolf and his horse drank their fill. They rested a while within the shade and gorged themselves on berries that grew along the banks.

Lone Wolf remounted and continued on his way beneath the tall pines. Streaks of sunlight, breaking through the dense canopy, filtered down onto the forest floor, casting glows amongst the shadows. The sweet smell of pine carried by the cool air seemed heavy enough to taste. The enchantment of this dark, tranquil forest reminded him of the Eastern Woodlands of his birth.

Lone Wolf stopped suddenly. Again, he heard a crackling rush. Looking behind, he saw the canopy of tall pines now ablaze. The Spirit of Fire had returned to unleash his fury, Lone Wolf thought. Towering flames raced through the closely spaced pines to where Lone Wolf and his horse watched in horror.

The flames leaped from treetop to treetop like a crazed squirrel. As fire spread within the dense canopy, blazing limbs dropped onto the dry forest floor, igniting the underbrush. A strong wind fanned the flames ever-faster toward Lone Wolf and his horse. Everything along the path they had just traveled was burning.

Flames now raged on both sides of them. Lone Wolf kicked his terrified horse, fleeing through the unburned forest ahead.

They made their way deeper into the woods until all was quiet again. There, a short distance ahead, was a stream of swiftly flowing water, foaming itself white as it cascaded over the rocks. They were finally out of reach of the Spirit's wrath.

Lone Wolf rode his horse into the middle of the stream and dismounted. After drinking their fill, he bathed himself and washed down Wacanga with the cool, refreshing water.

They rested again along the bank of the stream. His pinto cropped the succulent shoots that grew along the edge. Lone Wolf took smoked meat from his travel pack and ate. The sound of rippling water put his nerves at ease. Lone Wolf closed his eyes for a moment.

As he was about to fall asleep, he heard the crackling of flames, now louder than ever. He leaped out of the grass. The fire had managed to creep up on them. As the wind began to blow, the flames fanned out in all directions. Again, the Spirit was in pursuit.

Lone Wolf mounted up and rode back into the middle of the stream. There they would wait out the flames before reentering the forest.

But the Spirit of Fire would not be so easily outwitted, Lone Wolf realized. Burning branches from the tall pines began to drop into the streambed, falling to either side. Gusting winds blew a shower of embers all around Lone Wolf and his frightened horse. It was no longer safe to remain there in the stream. He rode over to the opposite bank where the flames had not yet reached the trees. Here they should be safe.

No sooner had he crossed the stream, than claps of thunder filled the skies. Lightning bolts flashed out of the clouds, striking the tops of the tall, yet unburned trees. Terror seized Lone Wolf. He saw the Spirit seated on his horse at the top of a ridge, hurling lightning bolt spears into the clouds above the trees. The Spirit had saved his best weapon until last. Soon the entire forest in front of Lone Wolf was engulfed in flames. Lone Wolf retreated back into the stream as fire closed in all around him.

Burning limbs snapped off the pines and fell into the water, from both sides of the stream. Lone Wolf maneuvered his horse back and forth, frantically dodging the falling limbs. The wind blew fiercer. Entire trees, all ablaze, began to fall across the stream, reaching to the opposite bank.

He had to act quickly or soon the Spirit of Fire would fulfill its promise and burn both him and his horse to 'cinders.' But there was no refuge left, now that the entire forest was engulfed in flames and the stream no longer safe.

Burning limbs dropped into the water, coming ever closer. His horse began to buck. Lone Wolf dismounted, took out a small fur from his travel pack, and drenched it in the stream. He tied the wet fur across the eyes of the animal. Wacanga immediately calmed down. Then he took out his bearskin coat and immersed it in the stream. He mounted his horse and, crouching low, pulled the drenched fur over his back to cover himself.

Lone Wolf turned Wacanga around to face the blazing forest through which they had first ridden. Realizing it was their last chance to save themselves, he kicked his now-blinded horse, driving him back into the inferno.

They rode between the trees, frantically weaving in and out to avoid the flames surrounding them on all sides. Lone Wolf guided the blinded animal around fallen limbs that lay smoldering on the ground, veering off at the last moment. He kept his body tight against Wacanga's, the still-wet fur now covering them both.

As they galloped deeper into the burning forest, flaming branches rained down on them from the overhead canopy. Hot embers fell onto Lone Wolf's back. The fur continued to provide protection. So long as it remained damp, Lone Wolf reminded himself, it would shield him and his horse. But the intense heat was beginning to dry out the fur.

Dodging falling limbs through the raging inferno, they pushed on frantically in their desperate flight. The scorching heat made it harder to breathe. The Spirit of Fire had unleashed all his fury.

Lone Wolf was sick with fear. If Wacanga stumbled over a fallen limb, his long journey could end here. Their charred bodies would be lost forever among the black ashes that surrounded them.

Riding deeper into the burning woodland, the flames grew smaller. The roar of the fire began to subside. They had traveled back to where the forest had nearly burned itself out. A short distance farther, the flames were gone. Lone Wolf stopped and looked around. Here was a death-like world, without color. On this scorched battlefield stood the smoldering hulks of once tall trees while on the forest floor lay the charred remains of their fallen comrades.

Lone Wolf's protective fur, having dried out, began to smolder. He now resembled the very Spirit who had unleashed all his fury against him. The cloak that had twice helped save his life, he discarded onto the ash-covered ground.

There, off to one side, was a gully. Lone Wolf rode into the depression and was surprised to find unburned grass within. He untied the blindfold from Wacanga and allowed him to feed.

They were now safe within the depths of their refuge. The blackened forest around them continued to smolder, burning itself out into harmless ash.

Lone Wolf laughed aloud:

"Spirit of Fire, what has happened to all your fury? Where are your raging flames, now that there is nothing left to burn?"

His horse looked at Lone Wolf and neighed. The two exhausted creatures lay down to rest, their bodies covered in black soot like the forest that surrounded them.

Lone Wolf fell into a deep sleep.

***

There, in a dream, Lone Wolf would see fire, from an earlier time, a raging fire about to consume the village of his people of the East, the Weckquasgeek.

Lone Wolf, his brother Rising Bear and his father Gray Eagle made their way through the woods, after having gathered with other tribes at the camp of the Siwanoy. They had met to expand the federation of Wappingers to include all their neighboring tribes, and to safeguard their remaining lands from the growing number of Dutch and English settlers.

Returning home, the three followed Wysquaqua Creek to where it flowed into the Mahikanittuc. As they reached the edge of the woods that bordered their village, they heard a loud commotion. Taking cover, they watched in horror:

Nearly, all the bark-covered wigwams had been set on fire by Dutch soldiers that had surrounded the village in a surprise attack. The militia, as it was called, was under the command of General Van der Hyl, whom they recognized immediately. The General gave orders to his soldiers to shoot their muskets into the village at anything that moved. Other soldiers crept up and set fire to the remaining wigwams, within which men, women and children soon became trapped.

["They demeaned themselves as soldiers and deployed in small bands, so that we got in a short time one dead and twelve wounded. Presently none durst come forth, keeping within the houses, discharging arrows through the holes. The General perceived that nothing else was to be done, and resolved to set the huts on fire, whereupon the Indians tried every means to escape, not succeeding in which they returned back to the flames, preferring to perish by the fire than to die by our hands. What was most wonderful is, that among this vast collection of men, women, and children, not one was heard to cry or to scream."][1]

Lone Wolf and his father, Gray Eagle, prepared to charge into the line of soldiers, hoping to send them into panic and so allow their people a chance to escape the flames. His brother, Rising Bear, remained behind, continuing his barrage of arrows to keep the Dutch pinned down.

With Gray Eagle in the lead, the two rushed from the woods, attacking the rear of the militia ranks. Suddenly a shot rang out. A cloud of smoke billowed from the end of a musket barrel. Gray Eagle was struck in the chest.

Lone Wolf knelt down next to the fallen body of his father.

Gray Eagle tried to speak, his voice faltering, "Lone Wolf, my son, I have been meaning to talk to you of a matter of great importance...."

His father died. He had taken his unspoken words with him to his grave. Those must have been the words

---

[1] *From an eyewitness account of the massacre of the Weckquasgeek, written by a Dutch militiaman and filed in 1647 at the Royal Library of The Hague, the Netherlands.*

that Lone Wolf had longed to hear. But the white man's musket had silenced his father forever.

Lone Wolf sprang to his feet in a wild rage. The militiaman who had shot his father was reloading his musket. With knife in hand, Lone Wolf leaped over the mound behind which the Dutch had taken cover. The butt of a musket struck him in the head. All became night as he fell helplessly to the ground.

When he regained consciousness, Lone Wolf found his hands tied behind his back. He now saw, for the first time, the devastation and carnage of the attack. Every bark-covered wigwam had been burned. The village had been reduced to smoldering piles of ash. Bodies of men, women and children, including that of his father, lay scattered over the ground. The stench of burning flesh hung in the air.

What remained of his people, those who had fled to the surrounding woods, were now rounded up and taken captive. Lone Wolf's mother was among them.

After they had finished scouting the woods for fugitives, the militia assembled what was left of the tribe. Lone Wolf was pushed into their ranks, his hands now untied. This would be the last time his people would ever see their ancestral lands.

The militia began to withdraw as the Weckquasgeek were turned over to a recently-arrived regiment of horse soldiers. The armed escort immediately forced his people to surrender all their furs. In their place they were issued cloth blankets, their only protection on the long march that now lay ahead.

The horse soldiers ordered the men, women and children, all on foot, to line up in single file. As they were about to leave, Lone Wolf looked back to the remains of the village where he had lived since his birth. He watched as the charred bodies of his people were thrown into a large pit that had been dug for a mass burial. There, too, was the body of his father, being dragged along the ground, then rolled over the edge of the pit.

Hatred for the white man burned in his heart as he watched helplessly.

"How could the Great Spirit allow such suffering to befall a faithful people who had always believed in Him?" Lone Wolf asked himself. "How could he allow such evil?" Then Lone Wolf recalled what had been taught by his ancestors since the long ago. "Not even the Great Spirit interfered with the free will of a mortal."

Lone Wolf surveyed the surrounding area, looking for the body of his brother, Rising Bear. He was nowhere to be seen. Perhaps he too had been killed and his body consumed by flames, or did he escape?

A gentle snow began to fall, extinguishing the smoldering embers of the wigwams. The flames had now been silenced, as had his people. The ashen remains of his village were soon covered under a blanket of white, leaving no trace that anything had ever existed there.

The horse soldiers ordered the long line of survivors to begin their march. Lone Wolf looked back for the last time to where his village had once stood. "I will never forgive the white man for what he has done. Never!"

The forced removal of the Weckquasgeek had begun. A long and arduous journey lay ahead, leading to captivity in a distant land. It was a journey that, for Lone Wolf, had begun in the raging flames of hatred, and would end in the bitter snows of revenge.

***

The rays of the sun lit up Lone Wolf's blackened face, waking him out of his sleep. He mounted Wacanga, the brown and white fur of its coat covered in soot. They rode up out of the gully that had served as their refuge for the night.

He made his way through the devastated forest. An acrid stench of smoke hung in the air. The smoldering remains surrounding him brought back

93

images from his dream of the night before — of his ancestral village burned to ashes, and the charred bodies of his people scattered over the ground. Lone Wolf seethed with hatred as the image of his dead father now flashed before him. He would never forget what the white man had done.

Retracing his path, he led his horse back through the burned forest, and into the stream where they had taken refuge the previous day. Looking down at his reflection, Lone Wolf saw his blackened face.

He leaped off his horse into the water, then began scrubbing himself, using sand from the streambed. Pulling Wacanga into deeper water, he washed off the heavy soot that covered the animal, revealing again the brown and white colors of its fur, now with burn scabs amongst the battle scars. The water around them was soon covered with floating soot. The soot was carried downstream by currents to where fallen trees still lay across the channel.

Lone Wolf mounted his pinto and continued on his journey. He rode out of the charred forest and into the woods beyond, where the pines were tall, and green, and sweet of smell, untouched by the Spirit of Fire. Through the depths of the virgin forests he steadily made his way to the East, to where the Great Spirit might finally reveal to him the last, unspoken words of his fallen father.

Chapter 10

Yellow Iron

Lone Wolf reached the top of a ridge, then pulled up suddenly on the reins of his horse. He recognized the distant river immediately. During the forced march to the reservation, he and the Weckquasgeek had passed by it.

The Missouri had its origins far in the Northern Plains, near the lands of the Blackfoot. Here at its southern end, it flowed through an area populated by white settlers. Lone Wolf would keep his distance, ever more cautious now that half his journey was behind him.

The fragrance of wild flowers hung in the air, evoking childhood memories of spring. The trees were filled with the songs of birds. They fluttered about making nests, each following the ancient call to continue its own species.

The crack of a rifle shot shattered the morning calm. Birds flew out of the treetops in a single rush. The round ricocheted off a limb above Lone Wolf's head. He took cover immediately, not knowing from which direction the shot had come. Could it be horse soldiers from a fort near the river?

Lone Wolf moved cautiously through the shrubs, searching for his attackers. The next round grazed him in the shoulder, knocking him to the ground. His head struck a rock, and all became night.

When he regained consciousness, he found himself alone, in front of a cave-like opening in the side of a mountain. The opening was framed in heavy timbers made from trees still wearing their bark. Both of Lone Wolf's wrists had been tied with rope to the handle of a wagon, made of the white man's metal.

He had been taken captive! The sweat of fear covered his face as he struggled futilely to free his hands. Who had done this?

He heard voices from deep within the cave. Two men walked out of the darkness. Each carried over his shoulder a strange double-pointed axe with a long wooden handle. Just as he feared - white men. They approached him cautiously, though his hands were still tied. One was an old man with white straggly hair and beard. The other had black stubble on his face and dirt-embedded creases around his eyes.

"What did I tell ya, Jedd," the old man said. "That Injun wasn't gonna die after all. Why he's too tough, even if he is gettin' old. Musta been in a lot of battles, too, from the looks of them scars across his chest."

"I hope you're right, Carson, that he's got strength left in him. I don't want him to eat our grub if he can't work hard for us."

"Sure I'm right, Jedd. We'll work him until we play out the mine. Then we'll turn him over to the regiment at the fort for a bounty, saying he's a renegade. We're makin' it at both ends. Ya can't beat that, Jedd, now can ya?" The old man chuckled.

"No, I guess not, Carson. But let's put him to work to see if he's strong enough to push the ore wagon out of the mine, once it's loaded. We got that pile of broken rock that's gotta be moved so we can get at the new vein of gold you say runs through the roof of the tunnel. I hope you're right, Carson, that you found the mother lode we've been searching for all this time!"

"Sure I'm right, Jedd. Just like I've been tellin' ya all along. You'll believe me when ya see those gold nuggets start fallin' out and makin' us rich." The old man's eyes filled with a crazed look as he spoke. He then turned toward Lone Wolf.

"See here, Injun, first ya gotta push this ore wagon into the mine, on these iron rails here, like this. It'll go straight, so ya don't have to steer. The ropes on your wrists are just long enough to let ya do your work. We gotta keep ya tied up, just in case ya might wanna leave us." Old man Carson laughed. He then leaned his weight against the ore wagon and moved it a short distance.

"Once it starts rollin', Injun, all ya gotta do is hold it back, so she don't go in too fast, understand, cause the rails slant downward into the rear of the mine. Goin' in, ya see, ain't bad at all, but comin' out is gonna be harder since you're goin' up hill a bit, and ya got a load of ore to push out. Now grab onto the long handle, like I'm doin', and push hard as ya can. Let me see ya do it."

Lone Wolf just stood there. He now understood his predicament. He was to labor for the two white men until exhausted, then turned over to the horse soldiers at the fort.

Annoyed that Lone Wolf did not respond to Carson's order, Jedd pushed him against the ore wagon. Lone Wolf fell to the ground. His hands, still tied to the handle, stretched over his head.

"You better work, like we tell you, redskin," Jedd warned, "or we're gonna bring you back to the fort, dead. Makes no difference to me. The bounty's still the same - fifty dollars, dead or alive!"

Lone Wolf realized the great danger he was in. It was inconceivable, he thought, that after the great distance he had already traveled, and after having confronted two spirits of nature, his journey could end here. He would never allow anyone, especially a white man, to prevent him from reaching his ancestral lands in the East. But he must bide his time, do what he was told, then strike quickly.

Lone Wolf leaned his weight against the handle, as Carson had shown, pushing the ore wagon toward the entrance of the mine. Shrills from the rusted wheels riding over the rails sent chills up his spine. Carson urged him on. Once in motion, the empty wagon continued to move under its own weight, down along the sloped rails and into the opening of the mine. Lone Wolf pulled on the handle to hold it back.

"That's right, Injun," Carson said. "Don't let her go down too fast, just make her move slow and steady. Ya see, Jedd, ya got to show him, 'cause he don't understand all our words."

The two prospectors each lit a lantern, then followed Lone Wolf into the mine. The tunnel was narrow, barely wide enough for the ore wagon to pass. The wagon came to an abrupt stop where the tunnel opened up into a cavern. A pile of broken rock had been placed at the end of the rails. Rays from the lanterns reflected off the specks of yellow iron within the ore.

"Ain't this beautiful, Injun?" Carson said. "Look here now at all this pretty gold. We're goin' to be rich, ain't we Jedd?" Jedd nodded his head.

"We're goin' to be filthy rich, especially with the mother lode I discovered this morning, Jedd." Carson looked up at the roof of the tunnel. As he held the lantern above his head, a vein of yellow iron, embedded in rock, glittered brightly.

"Sure, Carson, just as long as there's an even split between us, fifty-fifty, like you promised. I wanna get what's coming to me!"

"Don't fret none, Jedd. You're gonna get just what's comin' to ya. I promise."

The two eyed each other suspiciously. Lone Wolf sensed a growing danger.

Old man Carson picked up a piece of ore from the pile and dropped it into the wagon. A loud clang echoed through the tunnel.

"Now you do the same, Injun!" Carson ordered. "You load them rocks there into the wagon, just like I showed ya. They're in our way at gettin' at this new vein, so move out the whole pile."

Lone Wolf began loading the heavy stones. Carson came over to adjust the rope around his wrists, to give him more slack.

The prospectors started swinging their double-pointed axes into the roof of the tunnel. As they removed the surrounding rock, the vein grew larger.

"What I tell ya, Jedd," Carson said. "Look how far she runs! We hit the mother lode, for sure!"

The vein within the roof of the tunnel glittered more intensely, reflecting the lantern light. Nuggets of pure yellow iron now fell onto the floor of the mine as the prospectors picked away furiously. Lone Wolf looked on, becoming ever more anxious. Greed and mistrust seemed to take control of their spirits.

"Don't you go put none of those gold nuggets into your pockets, Jedd, ya hear," Carson warned. "Just remember this mine is my own claim. You're lucky I took you in as a partner."

"If it weren't for me giving you grubstake money after you ran out," Jedd said, "you'd never been able to come out here again to rework the mine."

"I would've gotten it from someone else," Carson said. "All ya came up with was a few measly dollars to buy beans and picks. Ya didn't even have enough for a mule to pull the ore wagon. Gotta use this Injun instead. So don't go pattin' yourself on the back, 'cause I'm the one who found this mine in the first place, and then the mother lode too. Just put all the gold over there in one pile, and I'll take care of the rest."

"What's an old man like you gonna do with all this gold anyway?" Jedd chided him.

"Never you mind 'bout that," Carson answered. "Sometimes an old man like me needs to have lots of gold, to make sure he's taken proper care of in his old age, when no one else wants him."

Lone Wolf continued loading the pieces of ore into the rail wagon, setting them down carefully so he could overhear the conversation.

"Ya know, Jedd, it's a good thing the Colonel at the fort lets us prospect on these reservation lands. We ain't supposed to be up here, so he's givin' us a break.

Too bad all the gold seems to be on Injun lands, in their 'sacred mountains.'"

"Didn't you tell me, Carson, that the Colonel asked the Bureau to redraw the boundaries of the reservation, so that the settlers can get all the good land, and the gold?"

"Yea, Jedd, that's right," Carson answered. "But we gotta take care of our Colonel soon as we get back. Some of this gold's gotta go straight into his pocket, or he'll let someone else jump my claim and prospect here in our place."

Lone Wolf listened to all their talk but pretended not to understand. He realized it was happening as before, back in the East, and on the reservation where his people had been resettled. The white man's greed for land, and now for yellow iron, had no limit. The tribes would be moved again to get them out of the way. The white man's word, and his written treaties, meant nothing!

The ore wagon was now filled. Lone Wolf leaned his weight against the handle, trying to push it along the rails that led out of the mine. It would not move. He unloaded pieces of ore and tried again.

Carson, noticing Lone Wolf was having difficulty, came over to help. Both men pushed against the handle, stretching their legs out behind them to lean their full weight against the heavy load. The ore wagon finally began to move, the shrills from its rusted wheels now louder than ever. Lone Wolf slowly pushed the wagon up the incline, then out of the mine into daylight. Carson followed.

"Right here, Injun. Take out the ore and stack it in a pile along this brook, just like I'm doing. Later we gotta check each piece to make sure there ain't any gold hidden inside."

Carson left Lone Wolf to unload the ore wagon by himself. After it was emptied, Lone Wolf pushed the wagon back into the mine. When he had finished a

100

second load, his back began to ache. The heavy work, he realized, would wear him down, and soon he would be too exhausted to escape. He could not keep up this pace much longer. But as the prospectors worked feverishly to expose the new vein of yellow iron, they created a second pile of stones larger than the first.

Lone Wolf labored for much of the day, loading the ore, pushing it out of the mine, unloading and stacking it by the brook. The pain in his back grew worse. But he must be patient and bide his time, he reminded himself. He knew he would have only one chance to escape.

After bringing the ore wagon back into the mine, Lone Wolf loaded it again.

"One more trip after this, Injun, and we'll let ya rest," old man Carson said, noticing his captive beginning to tire.

"We don't want ya to die on us, not right now," he laughed. "Not with all this work left to do."

As Lone Wolf pushed the heavy load up toward the opening, he looked outside. There at the edge of the clearing, just under the trees, was an animal. His heart began to race. It was Wacanga, its brown and white fur difficult to see within the shadows of the surrounding woods. His loyal pinto had found its way back.

Lone Wolf now was on the verge of exhaustion. He pushed the ore wagon out through the mine opening and toward the brook where the rails came to an end. He waited for his horse to come over to him, afraid to call its name and alert the prospectors inside the mine.

When Wacanga finally approached, Lone Wolf put his hands over its mouth, just as it was about to neigh.

Stretching out his tied wrists, he pushed the taut ropes against Wacanga's teeth, then snapped his own as though chewing.

The Pinto bit into the rope. How fortunate he was, Lone Wolf thought, to have a horse that was both the swiftest on the chase and the smartest of its kind.

The animal's powerful teeth began to chew through the ropes that had kept Lone Wolf bound to the ore wagon. The tough fibers did not cut easily. Lone Wolf grew more anxious. Carson called out to him from inside the mine.

"Hey, Injun, what's takin' ya so long? Hurry up and get back in here. Ya got one more trip to make before ya can rest."

The ropes finally snapped, freeing Lone Wolf's wrists.

The ore wagon, still loaded with rock, began to move under its own weight back toward the mine. It picked up speed as it rolled down the sloped rails, then disappeared through the opening.

Suddenly there was a loud clash, followed by rumbling. A cloud of dust billowed out of the mouth of the tunnel. Lone Wolf ran into the mine a short distance. Choking from the heavy dust, he waited for it to clear. He could see that the fast-moving ore wagon had derailed, flying off its tracks and striking one of the upright timbers that had supported the tunnel roof.

Part of the tunnel had already collapsed. Jedd was in the back reaches of the mine, out of sight. Old man Carson was lying on the ground nearby. He struggled to lift himself up. Lone Wolf turned to run.

Without warning, rocks began to rain down as the tunnel roof continued to collapse. Lone Wolf took cover within a recess in the wall. After all was quiet, he looked around. Stone rubble had covered Carson in a deep mound, leaving only his head exposed.

The collapsed roof had revealed, overhead, the largest vein of yellow iron that Lone Wolf had seen all day. It was this purest of glittering, yellow iron that now formed a mound of rubble, from the top of which Carson's head protruded.

"Help me, Injun!" Carson ordered. "Dig me out of here now!"

Lone Wolf stood there. A grin broke across his face.

"You got to dig me out before the rest of the roof caves in! Don't waste time looking for Jedd. I'll give you gold, if you help me."

How strange it was, Lone Wolf thought, to be conversing with this talking, bearded head protruding out of the mound of yellow iron.

"Look at how beautiful it is," Carson said, his crazed eyes reflecting the yellow glitter all around him. "But quick, dig me out, and I'll make you rich. I promise! I give you my word, Injun."

"The white man's word, the white man's promise are worthless," Lone Wolf answered. "They are as worthless as your written treaties, and as worthless as the yellow iron you dig out of the earth."

Carson looked surprised, hearing for the first time Lone Wolf's command of the white man's language.

From the back reaches of the mine came a loud rumbling, as more stones began to rain down. Lone Wolf turned and fled.

He ran through the tunnel, leaping between the rails. Fear raced through his mind — what an end this would be, to be buried alive within the bowels of the earth and to die slowly in the darkness, with Carson's protruding head for company. Faster and faster he ran. The rumbling grew louder as it closed in from behind.

No sooner had he reached the outside air, than the entire roof of the mine collapsed, sealing off the opening behind him. A cascade of falling stones spewed from the mouth of the tunnel, like vomit. A large cloud of dust billowed outward, enveloping Lone Wolf as he ran across the open ground.

When he was out of range, Lone Wolf stopped and waited for the rumbling to subside. He spit on the ground, his saliva contaminated with yellow dust.

All was now quiet. Then he heard Carson's faint voice from within, calling out to him.

The prospectors had been trapped, sealed forever within the depths of the mine, entombed in mounds of the purest of yellow iron. They now had all the riches they had lusted for throughout their lives, Lone Wolf thought, more than enough for each of them. But the sacred mountain would not be so easily defiled. It had swallowed them up.

***

Lone Wolf mounted his horse and rode down the mountain. As he made his way toward the prairie, he thought of his own people and how different they were from the white man. Since children, they had been taught to share with each other all that they had. For such was the will of the Great Spirit. And in that way of life, the old way, they found riches enough.

Lone Wolf patted his horse on the neck, grateful to him for once again having come to his rescue. The two loyal companions continued on their journey, riding into the forests and mountains through which they would pass but once.

Chapter 11

Spirit of the Winds

The mountains were now far behind as Lone Wolf and his horse made their way across the prairie. It was summer and the grass that surrounded them had grown tall on the treeless plains.

Gazing into the ever-distant horizon, Lone Wolf once again felt a sense of awe from the vastness of the land. The earth and sky seemed to go on forever, as endless and enduring as the Great Spirit himself — while one's presence on earth was but a fleeting moment.

There was growing stiffness in Lone Wolf's bones. Exhaustion from the long journey had begun to set in.

"Give me strength, Great Spirit," he prayed aloud, "that I may finally set eyes on the land of my birth, and on your sacred cliffs."

A shadow slowly swept over the ground. Lone Wolf looked up. The white-headed eagle had returned.

Suddenly, the figure of a man on horseback appeared in the distance. He kicked his mount and headed toward Lone Wolf. There was no place to take cover.

As the rider and horse crossed the prairie, they were enveloped within a whirlwind of dust that swirled upward from the ground. The whirlwind followed them at every turn, accompanied by a deafening roar.

The figure closed in rapidly, then stopped abruptly in front of Lone Wolf. Wacanga reared up.

Was he imagining this, Lone Wolf thought, or had fatigue finally affected his mind?

The strange rider raised both hands, revealing large feathers that grew from beneath his arms like the wings of a bird. As the whirlwind subsided, Lone Wolf could see that his horse, too, was covered with feathers in what appeared to be long, powerful wings folded tightly against its sides.

Lone Wolf stared in disbelief. What kind of creature was this? He tried to speak, but his words stuck in his throat.

"Why do you cross my domain?" the strange feathered figure asked. As he spoke, white vapor streamed from out of his mouth, forming a miniature cloud that hung momentarily in the air, then disappeared.

Lone Wolf finally answered. "But who, or what are you?"

"Who am I? What am I?" the specter said, his voice like the howling of the wind.

"Can you not see, mortal? Can you not hear? I am the Spirit of the Winds."

"Of what winds?" Lone Wolf asked.

"You fool of a mortal. I am the Spirit of all winds that blow from each corner of the earth. Such winds are of me and I of them. Now do you know who I am, Lone Wolf?"

"You must truly be a spirit," Lone Wolf acknowledged, "for you knew my name before I spoke it."

"No mortal need tell me his name. I have known you and your people since my powerful breath first blew across your lands. I am master of both the gentlest breeze that weaves through the grass, and the raging wind that rips trees out of the earth."

"Indeed," Lone Wolf answered. "I have seen the brutal strength of your winds, and trees uprooted despite their great size. You are a powerful spirit and, though your forces are unseen, their fury leaves its unmistakable mark."

"I need no mortal to advise me of my strength. You can tell me nothing at all that I do not already know, but one thing."

"Yes, Spirit?" Lone Wolf said, knowing the question that would follow.

"Why do you cross my domain?" the Spirit asked once again.

"I am returning to the land of my birth, far in the Eastern Woodlands," Lone Wolf answered.

"Notwithstanding, you may not pass this way. You must travel around. So be gone with you, or with one blast of my breath I shall sweep you and your mount off these plains."

The Spirit of the Winds began to turn around, preparing to ride off.

"Wait!" Lone Wolf shouted, startling the Spirit's horse. "Like the salmon returning to the waters of its birth, I do not have time to travel around obstacles that lie in my way."

"I have already spoken," the Spirit said. "You may not pass this way since you pay me no homage."

"I have wandered freely throughout my life," Lone Wolf said. "No man, nor spirit has ever stopped me."

"You speak boldly for one whose hair shows streaks of gray," the Spirit said. "You are no longer fit to challenge my brute forces, I the most powerful of all the spirits of nature. Now be gone with you."

"I shall pass this way," Lone Wolf said, "for I so will it, and no spirit may ever interfere with the free will of a mortal." "Since you are obstinate," the Spirit answered, "I will not stop you now. But you will have to face the most brutal of all my forces, one you have never seen before. Then we shall know whether your courage can match the bold words you speak so freely."

"So be it," Lone Wolf answered.

The Spirit of the Winds broke into a mocking laugh. A blast of air from his mouth sent Lone Wolf and his horse reeling backwards. The Spirit turned his horse around and rode off into the distance where he had first appeared. As he crossed the prairie, he stretched out his feathered arms. So, too, the wings of his horse unfolded from its sides and opened to their full extent, revealing their enormous size. Breaking into a gallop, both horse and rider began to lift off the ground. They soared into the air, rising steadily upward until they disappeared into the clouds. The howling wind that had followed them turned into a breeze, then faded away.

Had this all been a dream, Lone Wolf thought? Or had fatigue from his journey finally affected his mind? No matter, he would not be deterred from returning to the East—not by any mortal, nor by any spirit.

***

Lone Wolf continued across the prairie. A sea of grass now surrounded him on all sides, reaching to the underbelly of his horse.

He could see on the distant horizon the faint outline of a mountain, rising out of the plains. Standing by itself, with trees on its slopes, it appeared out of place. The eagle that had been flying overhead returned, then flew toward the mountain. Lone Wolf changed course and followed.

It was now midafternoon. Everything was quiet. The tall grass surrounding them did not move. No wind. No breeze. How strange, Lone Wolf thought. There was always a wind that blew across the prairies, though at times barely noticeable.

A dead silence hung in the air.

Lone Wolf stopped riding. He looked all around. The skies had turned gray. Behind him, in the distance, black clouds had begun to mass.

All was still. The crickets made no sound. It were as though there were no living creatures left in the world, only Lone Wolf and his horse.

They continued to ride through the tall, lifeless grass. Again they stopped and listened. There was an ominous feeling, as if time itself had stood still.

A breeze began to blow, gently bending the seed-laden grass downward in the direction of Lone Wolf's travel. Wacanga neighed. They rode on, through the sea of tall grass.

The breeze grew steadily stronger. The grass bent further, to half its height.

The breeze now became a wind. Lone Wolf turned around again. The sky behind him had turned black. The howling of the wind grew louder as it swept across the prairie.

Suddenly there was a strange sound, the likes of which Lone Wolf had never heard. From out of the prairie he had crossed the previous day came rumbling.

He could feel the earth trembling beneath him as the rumbling grew louder.

His horse became jittery, moving from side to side. Lone Wolf looked back yet again. There in the distance was an enormous black cloud that seemed to have dropped out of the sky. The cloud twisted in a violent, whirlwind motion, becoming narrower until it touched the ground. At its base dirt and rocks swirled at incredible speed as they were sucked upwards into its mouth.

Lone Wolf watched in terror. Never in his life had he seen anything like this. It were as though a giant demon had dropped out of the sky to devour everything in its path. Was this what the Spirit had threatened when he said, "the most brutal of all my forces"?

Fear shot through Lone Wolf's veins. He kicked his horse, causing the pinto to rear up before breaking into a gallop.

They ripped through the grass, fleeing for their lives. Lone Wolf crouched low against his horse, wrapping his arms tightly around its neck. The demon of the black cloud swept across the plains, revealing the massive size of its twisting funnel. It came ever closer, spreading more darkness over the earth along its ever-changing path.

Wild thoughts rushed through Lone Wolf's mind as he fled. The sky had spawned a huge, black snake, its voracious mouth about to swallow both him and his mount.

Lone Wolf and Wacanga raced across the prairie. The towering whirlwind pursued them relentlessly, changing its course to mirror their every move. As it closed in from behind, he felt the wind trying to pull him off his horse. It was about to devour them, Lone Wolf thought, together with its ravenous meal of rocks and earth. But in this vast, open land, there was no place to take cover!

Above the near-deafening roar, Lone Wolf heard laughter. There, overhead, was the Spirit of the Winds on his winged mount riding around the black funnel cloud, soaring along its swirling spiral, causing it to twist ever faster.

"Help me, Great Spirit!" Lone Wolf cried out, as his pinto slashed its way through the rippling sea of grass. "Deliver me from this demon of death."

Appearing from out of the dust was the shadow of a mountain, directly ahead, the same mountain toward which the white-headed eagle had flown earlier that day.

"Faster, Wacanga," Lone Wolf shouted, kicking his horse repeatedly. "Do not fail me now, or the demon will devour us both."

His horse, galloping at breakneck speed across the prairie, panted heavily. Blood began to flow from one of its nostrils. Lone Wolf feared he would soon ride his exhausted pinto into the ground.

Closing in from behind, the roar of the demon cloud became deafening. Rocks and sod, ripped out of the ground along its path, now swirled all around them.

Lone Wolf felt the force of the wind tugging ever harder on his back. He held on to Wacanga, his arms still wrapped tightly around its neck. Terror drove them on relentlessly in their frenzied flight.

All now seemed lost. Then only a short distance ahead, barely visible through the dust, the mountain appeared. Racing toward the foothills, Lone Wolf kicked his horse repeatedly, driving the frantic animal up onto the lower slope. Its back hoofs slipped over the loose rocks. It struggled frantically to regain its footing and climb higher. But where could they hide?

His exhausted pinto, on the verge of collapse, made its way onto the upper slope of the mountain.

"Help me, Great Spirit," Lone Wolf cried out again. "Deliver me from this demon of death."

Through the whirlwind of dust, Lone Wolf saw an opening in the side of the mountain. A cave! Stones, and now trees, swirled all around them as the demon of the black cloud was about to overtake them.

Kicking his pinto harder still, Lone Wolf drove the animal on relentlessly, draining from its exhausted body the last of its strength. Just as the black cloud was about to lift them both off the ground into its twisting funnel, they raced through the mouth of the cave. Into its depths they rode until reaching a cavern.

The deafening wind followed them in, forcing its way into the back reaches of the cave. Outside, huge stones and trees were hurled through the air like arrows, slamming into the side of the mountain.

Lone Wolf let loose of Wacanga's neck and slid onto the floor of the cave. Even here, far to the back of the cave, he could feel the demon's force as it tried to suck them out of their refuge.

The wind became deafening, then painful. Lone Wolf covered his eardrums with his fingers.

The wind grew stronger. A downpour of boulders and trees pounded the side of the mountain. The Spirit of the Winds had not yet finished with them. Suddenly, Lone Wolf felt terror as miniature dust-laden whirlwinds appeared, each moving haphazardly along the floor of the cave. The demon of the black cloud had spawned an army of warriors, made in its own likeness, but small enough to penetrate the depths of this refuge.

The mouth of the cave now filled with rocks and trees that had been hurled through the air. As the wind within the tunnel steadily weakened, the whirlwind warriors began to grow smaller. Then, all at once, they disappeared.

The deafening sound within the cave became faint. The opening had been sealed by the Spirit of the Wind's own force. They were now safe, deep inside the cavern.

Lone Wolf could hear the wind raging outside. The demon of the black cloud meandered about the mountain, searching futilely to get at the mortal who had dared to defy him. But he and Wacanga were now beyond his reach.

They both lay down to rest. The Spirit of the Winds had made no idle threat, Lone Wolf thought. He was, indeed, "the most powerful of all the spirits of nature." He had put them to the test, and had nearly prevailed.

Safe within the depths of the cave, the two exhausted creatures fell asleep while the storm continued to rage outside.

***

There, in a dream, Lone Wolf saw himself as a young boy, in the Eastern Woodlands, sitting around the campfire alongside his brother. Again, their father, Gray Eagle, prepared to tell a story to his two young sons:

"It was the Spirit of the Winds," he began, "who first brought the white man to our shores, and so changed the lives of our people, forever.

"A steady wind filled the tall sails of their wooden ship, enabling the white man to cross the endless waters. The winds of change had finally led the white man to our land.

"Until that time only our people, the Weckquasgeek, and the neighboring tribes of the Wappingers, lived along the Mahikanittuc. Since the long ago when our ancestors first entered the valley in search of prey, this land had been ours alone!

"The winds of change brought to our river the white man called 'Hudson,' whose ship of tall sails first appeared off the shore of our village.

"With him were others of his kind who came to stay, and who would gradually take from us all that had been ours. At first, we helped the white settlers and their families, bringing them food and furs to survive the winter until they could provide for their own needs. This generosity was soon forgotten.

"It began with the animals of the forests that had long sustained us — the beaver, elk and bear. The white man traded for these and other furs, to ship back to his homeland. Later he hunted for them himself. Soon the animals disappeared and, with them, our old way of the hunt.

"Then our health, a gift from the Great Spirit — this, too, they took from us. They brought with them their dreaded diseases, unknown to our tribe. In short time, sickness of all kinds attacked our people: smallpox, cholera, and measles. Our bodies were unaccustomed to such afflictions. These diseases swept through entire villages like a swarm of evil spirits, striking down men, women and children, young and old alike, until our numbers were reduced to less than that of the white settlers.

"Soon after, they traded to us the drink the white man called 'rum.' The proudest of braves fell victim to its curse, becoming its slave as it robbed them of both mind and spirit."

Young Lone Wolf listened quietly, together with his brother Rising Bear sitting alongside. The glows of the campfire reflected off their father's face, revealing the

113

sorrow that accompanied his words as he continued his story:

"And last they took our lands. Above all, the white man wanted the land. Our people did not understand what it meant to sell land to the white man, nor the greed within their hearts when they bartered for it. For one cannot sell land. It is an inheritance left to us by our ancestors since the long ago, an inheritance which we in turn must leave to our children, and they to theirs. No man can own land for his own use. Land is a sacred gift from the Great Spirit himself, to be used by all within the tribe to which it was first entrusted.

"To keep peace with the white settlers, and so that our generosity would not come into question, we traded small parcels of land with the understanding that it would be shared. Our people put their mark on the treaties and deeds that promised we could continue to hunt and camp there, as before.

"These treaties were soon broken, one by one, treaties that were supposed to last 'for as long as the sun shall rise.' The white settlers moved onto our lands and built their farms, with stone walls to keep others out. Their treaties meant nothing — their words and promises quickly forgotten. Their greed to own land grew as their numbers continued to increase. First the Dutch, then the English, piece by piece they took from us all of our ancestral lands: our villages, both summer and winter sites, our hunting grounds, our sacred places where we sought visions, even our ancient burial grounds. In the end we became strangers in our own homeland, in this valley that had been ours since the long ago."

Lone Wolf's father, with deepening sadness in his voice, now told of an encounter with the Dutch that led to war:

"On a tract of land that was once part of our hunting grounds, there was the farm of a Dutch settler, where fruit trees grew. 'Peaches' the white man called them.

"One day in late summer a young Indian maiden, about to be married, was wandering through the woods, gathering berries and nuts. She had planned to make a special treat for her husband-to-be.

"As she approached the edge of the forest, she saw a beautiful peach that hung from a tree just off the clearing. Reaching up on her toes, she picked the fruit and placed it gently into the basket with the rest of her berries and nuts. Without warning, a shot rang out. A musket ball struck her in the heart. The Dutch farmer, Hendrick van Dyck, had shot and killed her, for taking a peach from the tree that grew on land he called 'his property.' But it had always belonged to our people.

"Such is the greed and treachery of the Dutch and English settlers. They have taken from us all these things, but most of all they have taken our land, and with it, our way of life."

Lone Wolf's father then spoke his final words to his young sons:

"We must regain our ancestral lands. We must drive the white man back into the waters out of which he had first come, before it is too late and we, too, disappear from these forests like the animals we once hunted.

"And one of you, Lone Wolf or Rising Bear, shall become the Warrior Chief of our people, and upon him shall fall this sacred honor of leading our tribe and reclaiming the land that had always been ours."

His father's final words hung in the air like a heavy cloud. Which of these brothers was it to be, these brothers- of-the-same-birth? Young Lone Wolf had longed, since a child, for the honor of succeeding his father. As Warrior Chief of the Weckquasgeek, he would drive the white man forever from their tribal lands. And then he would win the seldom-heard praise of his father!

But his father would not yet say whom he favored to succeed him.

In early spring, Lone Wolf underwent the warrior's rite of passage. Proving his courage to the tribal elders, he earned the coveted eagle feather of a Weckquasgeek warrior. Soon after, his brother Rising Bear earned his as well.

The seasons seemed to pass quickly. By the following winter Gray Eagle had not made it clear which of his sons was to succeed him.

The two brothers competed relentlessly against each other, urged on by their father. Lone Wolf strove ever harder to prove himself.

During that winter, the main village of the Weckquasgeek was burned to the ground and Lone Wolf's father killed by the Dutch militia. So it was that his father would take his unspoken words with him to his grave. Only the Great Spirit could now answer that which had long burdened Lone Wolf's heart.

At the end of his dream Lone Wolf again saw the towering cliffs of the Mahikanittuc, and a lone eagle soaring above. It was there, in his ancestral lands, that the Great Spirit dwelt, and there that he must finally seek Him out.

***

The raging wind outside the cave had subsided.

Lone Wolf awoke out of his sleep and looked around the cavern which had served as a refuge throughout the night. His pinto was standing nearby.

He made his way toward the mouth the cave, then stopped suddenly. The opening had been filled with boulders and trees blown there by the demon of the black cloud. Fear raced through his veins.

Working in a frenzy to clear the opening, he could not move any of the heavier rocks or limbs. They had been sealed within the cave, he thought, like the two

116

prospectors who had been entombed alive with their mound of yellow iron. His refuge had now become his tomb.

The air within the cave was cold. Lone Wolf struck a flint, lighting a fire to keep warm. As the flames began to rise, he noticed the smoke being drawn to the back of the cave. There must be another opening, yes, another opening!

Lone Wolf took a sap-covered pine branch from the debris within the mouth of the cave and made a torch. The light from the torch revealed two small tunnels leading off from the rear of the cavern. He entered the one drawing the smoke, growing more hopeful as he followed it to its end.

Directly overhead in the roof of the tunnel was an opening through which a beam of light penetrated the darkness. But the opening was out of reach and far too narrow to provide an escape for Lone Wolf. His heart sank.

Retracing his steps back to the main cavern, he followed the second tunnel. He walked slowly, realizing this was his last hope.

"Help me, Great Spirit," Lone Wolf prayed aloud, his voice echoing through the back reaches of the cave. "Help me, Father of all spirits."

He continued down the second tunnel, ever slower, afraid of what he might find. The tunnel opened up into another cavern.

At first it was so faint, he barely noticed it. Then the sound of trickling water grew louder. As Lone Wolf reached the back of the cavern, his torch about to burn out, there within the floor he saw a pool of water. The water was dark, except in one area near the bottom where traces of sunlight penetrated from the side.

He stood a while, staring into the dark abyss. "You can not let me die like this, Great Spirit. Not like this!" If the opening below were not large enough, they would surely drown. But there was no other way out.

Lone Wolf led his horse back into the cave a short distance, then turned him to face the pool. He mounted Wacanga and, kicking his heels into its sides, drove the animal toward the pool. They plunged headlong into the dark water, and sank to the bottom.

Submerged within the frigid waters, his horse fought its way through the murky depths to where sunlight had managed to penetrate. Lone Wolf kicked his mount harder, urging him on before they both ran short of breath.

As they struggled frantically toward the light, the water became clouded from agitation. It was harder to see. Lone Wolf began to panic. Then there, brightly illuminated, was an underwater opening within the side of the mountain. But was the submerged opening large enough for them to swim through?

Lone Wolf and his horse thrashed furiously to pass through the jagged opening, trying once and then again. They scraped themselves repeatedly against the sides. On their third attempt, they finally cleared the underwater cavern, then pushed ahead into the bottom of a lake outside the mountain. His horse paddled steadily, rising through the frigid waters as Lone Wolf held on tightly. Gasping for breath, they finally broke through the surface of the lake, into sunlight. How sweet was the pine-scented air that now filled their lungs.

They swam with barely strength left to reach shore, then collapsed on the embankment. Near exhaustion, the two rested a while along the edge of the tranquil lake. Lone Wolf lay on his back, outstretched on the grass. He gazed up at the now-peaceful sky, admiring the airy wisps of clouds that drifted by from time to time, afloat on an endless sea of blue. How good it was to be alive! How good to see the sun and sky for one more day!

After resting a while, Lone Wolf mounted his pinto and continued on his way, relieved to leave behind the mountain of refuge that had nearly become his tomb. He looked back one last time to the prairie behind him, noticing the deep scar across the grasslands where the demon of the black cloud had gouged out a reckless trail of destruction, devouring everything along its path.

The Spirit of the Winds had, indeed, put him to the test, Lone Wolf thought. The winds of this Spirit had once driven the white man's ships of tall sails to the shores of the Weckquasgeek, bringing an end to his people as they once were. But Lone Wolf had done battle against this same Spirit and its awesome forces. He had been tested and, again, he had proven himself.

The winds had now subsided, except for a gentle breeze from the East. Lone Wolf and his loyal pinto continued on their journey, slowly making their way across the vast prairie.

Ahead lay the Eastern Woodlands and the Mahikanittuc River, where Lone Wolf's people once ruled before the arrival of the white man. But what other obstacles remained in his way, Lone Wolf wondered, before he could finally set foot on his ancestral lands? And was it possible that his brother, Rising Bear, might still be there, after all this time?

Then he heard, again, the call of distant drums from out of the East.

Chapter 12

The Mahikanittuc

It was late summer when Lone Wolf and his horse crossed what was left of the eastern prairies. He had traveled a great distance. Soon he would reach one last horizon, he thought, then finally set eyes on the land of his birth. But again Bird Rattler's warning came to mind—the white man now ruled all of the Eastern Woodlands. Lone Wolf had always known his life would be in certain peril once he returned. Nonetheless, he remained determined. He would overcome any obstacle in his way, including the hated white man.

As he journeyed farther East he noticed, every so often, a homestead belonging to white settlers. When he had passed through these lands thirty snows before, they were nowhere to be seen. Now they had begun to move west, making their presence known in their usual manner, by fencing off the land they claimed for themselves. Their numbers had grown, he realized, and so must his vigilance during this final leg of his journey.

Attempting to avoid an area populated by white settlers, Lone Wolf now headed south. In the distance he saw a field of cotton being worked by black slaves — men, and women with their children, all toiling in the sun as they picked each white cluster by hand. He knew immediately, for back in the Eastern Woodlands he had seen wealthy Dutch landowners use black slaves on their farms. How cruel was the white man, he thought, to enslave such a kind and gentle people. But he must be on his way before he himself was taken captive.

Along the streams, through forests, and into uninhabited mountains Lone Wolf and his horse pushed on with single purpose. They passed, in turn, through the river valleys of the Ohio, Susquehanna, and

Delaware as they journeyed ever closer to the Eastern Woodlands. The wind now carried with it the fragrance of oak and maple that had once been familiar to him. With the passing of each day, he grew more anxious.

Lone Wolf entered the mountainous area the white man called the 'Hudson Highlands.' It had once been a battleground between his people and the hostile Mohawks to the north. The sun was about to set when Lone Wolf reached the top of a hill. Through an opening in the trees, he saw the rays of the sun reflecting off the waters of the Mahikanittuc below. His heart raced as he felt a renewed vigor in his body.

Stretching above his horse, he saw the beloved river of his youth. On the far shore were the tree-covered hills of his ancestral lands.

Lone Wolf dismounted and knelt on one knee, burying his spear point into the ground. Holding onto the shaft, he prayed in silence to the Great Spirit.

He would camp here for the night, along the western shore. Tomorrow, early, he would cross over the Mahikanittuc, returning at long last, to the land of his birth.

***

The rays of the rising sun broke over the wooded hills that lined the distant shore. Lone Wolf awoke immediately. It had not been a dream after all! Below stretched the Mahikanittuc. He now saw it in the full light of morning. How beautiful. But the river was much wider than he had remembered. He felt a strange uneasiness at the prospect of crossing it, and setting foot on his ancestral lands.

Lone Wolf and Wacanga slowly made their way down the hillside and onto the shore. The Mahikanittuc was calm. As he stepped into its waters, he bathed his face. He then drank from it, but spit it out immediately.

121

The brackish taste reminded him that the river flowed into the endless waters to the south.

He and Wacanga waded through the water, both able to reach bottom. For a distance off shore, the river remained shallow. As it became deeper, they began to swim, with Lone Wolf alongside his horse.

They swam farther out, toward the middle of the river. Large sturgeons appeared in the waters nearby, some as great in length as a man is in height. Lone Wolf leaned on his horse for support.

When they reached the middle of the river, the currents suddenly began to shift. First, they were swept downstream by the river's flow of fresh water from the north. Then the incoming tide, from the endless waters to the south, carried them back upstream. Turbulence developed where the two opposite flows collided, creating eddies and whirlpools.

Both Lone Wolf and his pinto began to struggle, fighting the waves to avoid being swept away by the ever-shifting currents. The tidal surges moving upriver continued their assault against the fresh water flows moving downriver in what was now a battlefield of swirling eddies. Lone Wolf had been caught at the worst possible time, in the worst possible reach of the river.

How foolish not to have remembered, Lone Wolf realized. Mahikanittuc—'the river that flows both ways.'

"Great Spirit," Lone Wolf cried out as he was being tossed about in the rough waters. "Is this what You had planned all along? To have me travel a great distance, only to drown while in sight of my ancestral lands?"

At that moment a white-headed eagle appeared overhead.

Lone Wolf, near exhaustion, held on tightly to his horse. He let loose of its bridle rope for a moment, trying to hook his arm around its neck. His arm slipped off the wet fur. The surging currents carried him upstream a short distance. He bobbed up and down in the waves.

Only his head was visible. The swirling waters tried to pull him under.

"Help me, Wacanga!" Lone Wolf cried out.

His horse neighed. Pumping its powerful legs, it fought against the shifting currents to where Lone Wolf was struggling to stay afloat.

Fear seized Lone Wolf as his head went under the surface of the water a second time. With all his remaining strength, he flailed his arms against the waves, trying to keep his mouth above water. He would fight to the very last, he promised himself. But now all seemed hopeless.

Wacanga thrashed its way through the water, swimming ever closer. Just as Lone Wolf was about to go under, he reached out and wrapped his arms around Wacanga's neck.

Looking up into the face of his pinto, Lone Wolf saw blood flowing from both nostrils. He felt panic. If his horse gave out now, his journey would end here, in the middle of the river.

The turbulence became stronger as the tidal surges from the south continued to collide with the river flows from the north.

Again, the ever-shifting currents carried them downstream, then back upstream.

The pinto, with Lone Wolf hanging tightly onto its neck, thrashed furiously against the flows. Its powerful but tired legs continued to fight the currents, bringing Lone Wolf ever closer to shore.

Lone Wolf, totally exhausted, could not keep himself afloat. He hung off Wacanga like a dead weight, making its task more difficult.

His pinto continued to struggle. It steadily made its way closer to land. The flow of blood from its nostrils grew heavier.

As they neared the easternshore, the water became shallow enough for both to reach bottom. Yet Lone Wolf continued to hold onto his horse.

The rush of blood out of the animal's nostrils began to flow onto Lone Wolf's face. He finally let loose his grip, then found his footing as he touched bottom. Suddenly Wacanga neighed and collapsed into the water.

Lone Wolf, standing in the shallows, looked down at the body of the brown and white pinto now floating in the water. His faithful companion of the trail was dead. Lone Wolf wept for the horse he had always loved.

He thought back to all of life's journeys the two had shared, the nameless mountains and forests through which they had ridden, the distant horizon luring them ever onward.

He recalled the times during this last journey that his loyal pinto had come to his rescue when all seemed lost. He remembered the challenges, both of mortal and spirit alike, that they had faced together: the Kutenai; Sergeant Cody and the horse soldiers; the prospectors; and the three unrelenting spirits of nature. He remembered how he and Wacanga had struggled to overcome every obstacle that had crossed their path. And he knew, in his warrior's heart, that the courage of his beloved pinto was as great as his own. In the end Wacanga had sacrificed its life to save Lone Wolf's, when only a short distance from the shore it would never reach.

Crouching into the water, Lone Wolf pushed the floating body of his horse back toward the middle of the river. The strong currents soon carried it farther out. He watched it float slowly to the south,past the wooded hills on the far shore. The river's own flows had finally overcome the tidal surges that until now had denied it passage.

The currents grew swifter. The floating body of his pinto was carried steadily down river, becoming ever smaller until it disappeared into the endless waters beyond.

Lone Wolf wept again.

Struggling through the shallow water, he made his way to the embankment of the eastern shore. There he collapsed to the ground and fell into a deep sleep.

In his dreams Lone Wolf saw a salmon returning to the waters from which it first drew life, leaping to overcome the many obstacles along its way.

He, too, had returned at long last, to the place of his birth.

Chapter 13

In Search

An eagle flies above the river toward the eastern shore. On the sand below lies the figure of a man, returned at last to the land of his birth.

***

The sound of waves lapping against the rocks woke Lone Wolf from his sleep. Exhausted from his near-fatal crossing, he had slept through the day and into the following morning.

Lone Wolf picked himself up off the sandy shore. He looked downstream to where he had last seen his horse being carried away by the currents. The river was calm, giving no hint of the great fury of which it was capable.

He found his spear floating along the shore. Now without a horse, he set out into the forest on foot, as he had done as a youth. He was once again a Weckquasgeek.

Hoping to avoid the white man's settlements along the lower reach of the river, Lone Wolf headed deeper into the forest. Hidden within the dense growth of trees, he cautiously made his way south, toward what had once been the site of his village.

With the passage of time, Lone Wolf had all but forgotten the beauty of his ancestral lands. How enchanting were these ancient forests, with their secluded hollows and shaded streams.

As he walked through the wooded interior, he noticed areas where trees had been cleared by the Dutch and English. Since he had left these lands long ago, white settlers had encroached deeper into the forests that were once the tribal hunting grounds of his people. The cleared areas had become farms. All were bordered by stone walls that followed the contours of the rolling hills — walls that marked each white man's own 'property.'

There were many more of them now, Lone Wolf realized. He must be ever more cautious, or he would be seen and taken captive.

Lone Wolf grew anxious as he drew closer to the site of the village where the lodge of his family had once stood. There he would seek a vision of his father. No doubt the spirits of the dead would return from time to time to visit the places where they had experienced so much earthly happiness. He must hurry, then, so as not to chance missing him.

The village of his birth, he reminded himself, had long been burned to the ground. It had been situated on a level ridge overlooking the Mahikanittuc, its location providing a vantage point from attacks, as well as a commanding view of the river with its towering cliffs on the far shore. Alongside the village, below the ridge, flowed Wysquaqua Creek. A year-round source of fresh water, it emptied into the Mahikanittuc a short distance beyond.

Lone Wolf searched the woods a while before he was able to locate the northern branch of the Wysquaqua that would lead him to the village. After drinking from its waters, he followed the stream until it joined with the southern branch, from which point they flowed as one to the west. From here, the combined stream meandered through the woods, cutting a channel through a limestone gorge. He steadily made his way along the streambed.

A short distance beyond the gorge, Lone Wolf left the stream. Climbing up to the level ridge above, he finally reached the site where the village of the Weckquasgeek had once stood. He felt a rush of blood.

The clearing was overgrown with weeds, as though there had never been any encampment there at all.

The moment he set foot on the site, he tripped. Down at his feet he saw the remains of a charred wood post. Images suddenly flashed through his mind: his village under attack; bark-covered wigwams in flames; women and children trapped within their burning lodges. Hatred for the white man flared anew in Lone Wolf's heart.

He walked through the weeds to the outskirts of the village, then stopped suddenly. The ground there had settled. Once again images flashed through his mind: the Dutch militia rounding up survivors; charred bodies of his people being thrown into a pit; his slain father dragged along the ground. And once again hatred of the white man flared in Lone Wolf's heart as he looked down to where the ground had settled.

He knelt on one knee, holding onto his spear.

"I have returned, Father. It has been over thirty snows since being driven from these lands. I have not forgotten. I pray for you to appear and quiet the longing in my heart, that I may finally hear the words you took to your grave."

There was silence, except for the wind as it blew from across the Mahikanittuc.

Again, Lone Wolf prayed for his father to appear. And again there was only the wind.

Perhaps where his family's lodge once stood, Lone Wolf thought, he would see a vision of his father. Surely his spirit must visit there from time to time.

Walking to the opposite side of the village, Lone Wolf noticed a mound, nearly as tall as himself. The mound was made of discarded shells of oysters eaten by his people over many generations. He remembered having eaten his share of oysters harvested from the river below. A distance beyond the mound he found the towering oak which had shaded his family's lodge.

Searching the ground beneath the tree, he discovered remains of the campfire that had once burned within the lodge. There, nearly covered by weeds, were the blackened stones, still in a circular pattern as they had originally been laid. This was the campfire that his mother had kept supplied with wood, and his father with an abundance of game from the forest, the same fire that had warmed their lodge during the long winter nights when the Spirit of the Snows roamed across the land. For a fleeting moment he saw himself there as a young boy, asleep close to the fire, wrapped in a bear fur. Lying nearby within the lodge would have been his father, mother and brother. They were all gone now. All that remained were the blackened stones, nearly covered by weeds, and the fading memories of his youth. How foolish to have come back here at all!

Lone Wolf walked over to a fallen tree and sat down to rest. He looked around the empty campsite. His mind wandered freely, carrying him back further in time. Suddenly appearing from the shadows, were the wigwams that had once stood there. From out of the wigwams the ghosts of his people emerged. They were soon busy in the activities of everyday life. There were the children playing and running; the women fetching water and firewood, cooking meals; and the men returning from the hunt, laden with deer and turkey. But the area around his own campfire was deserted. Where were the spirits of his father, and of his mother and brother? No matter how hard he prayed, they would not appear.

The images of his people and of their lodges faded back into the shadows. Lone Wolf felt disappointment. He got up and made his way toward the surrounding woods. A strange sense came over him. He turned to look back one last time.

There, under the oak, seated outside their lodge, were his father, mother, and brother. He could see them clearly, except for his father whose back was turned towards him.

Lone Wolf called out to them, but they seemed not to notice him. They continued to talk amongst themselves.

He ran through the tall weeds to where they were seated. His father stood up, his back still turned, then made his way into the surrounding woods. Lone Wolf chased after him. His father began to run, maintaining a pace that kept him just beyond reach.

Through the woods, along the streams, leaping over fallen trees, Lone Wolf raced after the fleeing figure of his father. "Father, wait for me, I beg." They ran ever faster. Near exhaustion, Lone Wolf tripped and slid face down onto the leaf-covered ground. Looking up, he saw the image of his father disappear into the dark woods.

Why had his father's back been turned towards him, never to show his face? And why had he fled? Lone Wolf wished only to speak to him. What was the meaning of this vision?

Picking himself up, Lone Wolf searched the surrounding woods where he had last seen the fleeing image of his father. There were no tracks.

Deep within the woods, Lone Wolf found a secluded area surrounded by bushes. He would sleep here the night, then in the morning again seek out his father's spirit. He would search in the cherished places of his boyhood memories.

***

The rays of the sun broke through the forest canopy. Lone Wolf awoke and returned immediately to the site of his village. No sooner had he entered the overgrown area than he knelt on one knee and prayed:

"Father, I have traveled far to seek you out. Return from the Spirit Land, now, so that I may finally see your face and hear the words you took to your grave."

There was silence, except for a gentle wind that blew from across the river. The wind carried with it winged seed pods from a maple tree. The falling pods reminded Lone Wolf of the first snowfall of winter. Yes, an omen, he thought. The snow-covered hills of his youth. That would be where he would look next, among the memories of boyhood and of winters long past.

On the opposite side of the ridge was a gently sloped area that led down toward a pond. Here along this treeless hill young Lone Wolf and other children of the tribe would come in winter to sleigh.

Walking to the top of the hill, Lone Wolf looked down the slope. It was covered in snow. A vision!

He saw himself there, as a young boy, playing in the newly-fallen snow. And there, too, was his father, standing in the distance near the bottom of the slope.

The young boy climbed to the top of the slope to try out his sled — its runners made from the antlers of a deer. Below his father waited for him. The two were the only figures on the snow-covered hill.

Beginning his long slide, the boy shouted in excitement as the sled glided swiftly over the blanket of snow.

Lone Wolf ran down the hill. Stopping to catch his breath, he stood midway between his father and the specter of his youthful self. Perhaps if he intercepted the sled, his father would come over to him.

The boy, gliding steadily down the slope, passed straight through Lone Wolf as though he were not standing there at all.

When he reached the bottom of the hill, the boy sprang from his sled and, with outstretched arms, ran toward his father. His father knelt down and embraced him. They then walked away, hand in hand.

Lone Wolf cried out.

"Father! Father! Do you not recognize me? It is I, Lone Wolf your son, now grown to manhood. Wait for me, I beg! I must speak to you."

As Lone Wolf headed across the expanse of snow, the two figures began to flee. He ran after them.

He reached the area where they had been only moments before. There were no footprints in the snow. They had vanished.

Lone Wolf wept. How he yearned to feel his father's embrace for one last time, in this most lonesome winter of his long and restless life.

But why had the specter of his father fled, when all Lone Wolf wanted was to speak to him?

Bird Rattler's words of counsel returned to mind. It was the Great Spirit who commanded all the people of the past, and who alone could send Lone Wolf's father to him.

Chapter 14

The Sacred Cliffs

The rays of the setting sun filtered through the trees, illuminating the forest floor. As he looked toward the western sky, Lone Wolf felt drawn to the river.

Making his way cautiously through the woods, he reached a hill covered with heavy brush. With his stone knife, he hacked an opening through the thicket, then climbed to a secluded ridge that overlooked the river. He had found the ridge-of-the-three-pines where, as a boy, he would retreat from time to time to seek visions. There, on the distant shore, towering above the river, were the weathered cliffs of the Mahikanittuc.

It had been over thirty snows since Lone Wolf had seen them last. He himself might have aged, and the joints of his bones now stiff, but the ancient cliffs were as he had always remembered —forever unchanged.

The setting sun illuminated the western sky in crimson and gold. For a moment, the sun seemed to touch the top of the cliffs, then slowly disappeared as though lying down to rest.

The words of his father, which Lone Wolf first heard as a child, came back to mind:

"The sacred cliffs of the Mahikanittuc are the resting place of the Great Spirit. At the end of each day, after roaming the earth, He returns to this very place to make camp for the night. So, it has been since the beginning of time. There, amid the ancient cliffs on the far shore, is where the Great Spirit dwells."

Lone Wolf knelt on one knee, burying his spear point into the ground. He prayed to the Great Spirit to send from the distant shore the vision of his father that he had sought throughout his life.

During the night, and all of the next day, Lone Wolf remained on the secluded ridge. He fasted and prayed.

"Send the spirit of my father, I plead, and command that he not flee, so I may finally speak to him."

All was quiet, except for the wind.

Lone Wolf continued his vigil on the ridge-of-the-three-pines. The sun again set down to rest atop the cliffs on the far shore. And again he prayed:

"Since you send no vision of my father, Great Spirit, reveal yourself instead. Speak to me, as my father never did."

All was quiet.

Standing at the very edge of the ridge, Lone Wolf cried out:

"Great Spirit! Why have You forsaken me? I am Lone Wolf, a warrior without a people, the last of my kind. Speak to me, before I die, the words my father took to his grave."

All was quiet, except for the wind as it blew from the distant shore.

The ancient cliffs remained, as they had always been, forever silent.

***

After his long vigil and fasting, Lone Wolf returned to the hunt. He was famished. Within a short time, he picked up the tracks of a deer.

Stalking his prey through the undergrowth, he spotted a buck. His mouth began to water as he thought of feasting on roasted venison, cooked over an open fire to a crisp brown.

Crouching behind a bush, he looked down to avoid stepping on branches that would scare off his prey. He tested the wind direction, careful that his scent not be carried back.

Lone Wolf closed in for the kill.

Wait! Had the fasting affected his mind?

Directly in front, a short distance away, he saw another hunter, dressed in buckskin and head roach — a Weckquasgeek like himself, stalking the same deer. Could it be that one of his own people still remained in the forest?

Lone Wolf crept up behind the hunter. When within arm's reach, the figure turned around. They stared into each other's face. Blood surged through Lone Wolf's veins.

"Father! At long last, the Great Spirit has sent you!"

His father immediately turned his back and fled into the forest.

Lone Wolf chased after him. There was no way he would allow the specter to escape again, now that he had finally seen his face.

Through the woods, across streams, into gullies, step for step, Lone Wolf gave chase to his father's fleeing image. He called out to him repeatedly.

"Speak to me, Father, I beg you!"

But the specter of his father continued to flee.

"Stop, Father, for the sake of a son who loved you during your earthly life!"

As he ran, branches whipped across Lone Wolf's face, scourging him until he bled. But no blood dripped from the figure of his father just a short distance ahead.

Faster and faster his father made his way through the forest. Lone Wolf kept pace, panting harder, getting short of breath. Suddenly Lone Wolf collapsed from exhaustion and fell headfirst onto the ground. Sliding over the damp leaves, he came to rest at the base of a tree.

Lone Wolf saw the figure of his father, just a short distance ahead, disappear again into the shadows of the forest.

He wept.

"Why do you weep, brave warrior of the Weckquasgeek?" came a strange voice.

Lone Wolf, still lying on the ground, looked around and saw no one. Surely he must be losing his mind, he thought.

He heard the voice again, coming from overhead.

As he looked up, he caught a glimpse of a man's feet, suspended from the tree above. He could not believe his eyes.

Overhead, hanging by his outstretched arms lashed to the limbs of the tree, was the figure of a man. Blood flowed from his hands, and from a spear wound in his side.

Who was he, Lone Wolf wondered, this stranger who spoke his own Algonquin tongue as well as any, and wore the loincloth of a Weckquasgeek? And why was he suspended in torment, as in the gazing-at-the-sun ritual—practiced by tribes of the Northern Plains to bring one's soul closer to the Great Spirit?

"To what tribe do you belong?" he asked the outstretched figure overhead. His sorrow-filled face, partly in shadow, was difficult for Lone Wolf to see.

"I belong to all tribes, to all tribes that ever were, and that will ever be."

"Has the Great Spirit sent you? Are you the vision I have sought?" Lone Wolf asked.

"I have been sent by the Great Spirit, as a father sends his son. I am of the Great Spirit, and He is of me. I come to you, as I come to all those who seek the Truth."

Lone Wolf knelt on one knee before the suspended figure, burying his spear point deep into the ground.

"Tell me, then," Lone Wolf asked, "why does my father's spirit flee from me, when I wish only to speak to him?"

"It is from the feelings you carry in your heart that he flees."

"What feelings," Lone Wolf asked, "for I carry nothing but love and esteem for my father."

"There are other feelings...of bitterness and resentment you still carry for your brother, Rising Bear. They are what drives away your father's spirit, and the reason he has led you to me."

"How would you know of such feelings toward my brother, which I have told to no one?"

"I know all, even the darkest of thoughts hidden within a mortal's soul. For there is nothing, Lone Wolf, nothing at all I do not know."

Bird Rattler's warning now returned to mind. There was nothing one could hide from the Great Spirit, "for He knows the innermost, darkest thoughts of us all."

For certain, then, Lone Wolf thought, the stranger before him must have been sent by the Great Spirit himself. For how else would He know the feelings long buried in his heart, feelings confided to no one, not even to Bird Rattler.

"If my father flees from me, why then will the Great Spirit not reveal himself instead?" Lone Wolf asked. "I have prayed to Him throughout all my life, and have carried love in my heart for Him."

"How can you love the Great Spirit, whom you have never seen, and not love your own brother with whom you once shared your youth?"

Lone Wolf did not answer. He sat down on a nearby rock to collect his thoughts. As he looked up at the Spirit hanging from the tree, he saw suffering in his face.

"Can I cut you down?" Lone Wolf asked, feeling pity.

"No. This sorrow I bear is my destiny, as sorrow comes to all mortals within their own lives. You can lessen it greatly, however, if you were to seek out the Great Spirit."

137

"I have sought Him out, high above the sacred cliffs, where He lies down to rest each night. Yet I have not found Him, despite my prayers and fasting."

"You must first seek Him out in your heart," the Spirit answered. "For it is there, when one is at peace with himself and with his brother, that the Great Spirit dwells."

"But I believe, as my people have taught since the long ago, that He dwells beyond," Lone Wolf answered, pointing with his spear. "There, on the sacred cliffs of the Mahikanittuc, in his ancient, stone lodge."

"Indeed it is so, but He will never be known to you until you have allowed Him to dwell within your own heart as well," the Spirit answered. His voice was like a gentle whisper that reminded Lone Wolf of the wind that blew from across the river from time to time.

"To do this," Lone Wolf asked, "should one suspend himself from a tree, as you have done, piercing the flesh while enduring great pain? Or does one seek out a vision, high on a secluded ridge? Or can He be found in dreams?"

"None of these," the Spirit answered. "The jealousies and hatreds that burden one's soul must first be driven out, like a medicine man expelling evil spirits from the sick. And so, Lone Wolf, you must first make peace with your brother, by letting go of the bitterness and resentment you have long felt towards him."

"Am I not justified in my feelings against my brother, who sought to take from me the headdress of Warrior Chief? I had proven myself to all within our tribe, yet he continued in his pursuit of what was rightfully mine, until it was too late. How can I forgive him for such an injustice, and for trying to win the favor of my father over me?"

"You cannot judge your brother so harshly," the Spirit answered, "since you do not know the burdens he carried within his own heart, as all mortals do. Judge him not, or else the Great Spirit will so judge you. And forgive him as well, for any hurt or injustice you believe he may have caused you. Do this and the Great Spirit will forgive you, in turn, when your time has come to cross over to the Spirit Land."

"But even if I wanted to, my brother must have met his fate long ago at the treacherous hands of the white man, as my father did."

"Nonetheless, you must seek out your brother to see if he still walks amongst the living, then make your peace with him once and for all. If not, you must find his burial place and pray for forgiveness from his weathered bones."

The Spirit was asking too much, Lone Wolf thought. How could he ever forgive his brother. After the passage of so much time, this was too difficult. Again he had confronted a spirit, and again he was being put to the test. But this time as never before.

"Do you believe yourself worthy to enter the Spirit Land, and to join there the people of the past?" the Spirit asked, sensing the strife within Lone Wolf's heart.

"Yes!" Lone Wolf answered without hesitation. "Have I not proven myself throughout my life, as a Warrior Chief? Have I not always led my people to victory on the fields of battle, too numerous to recall? How many acts of courage are necessary for the Father of all spirits to deem me worthy?"

"This is not enough, Lone Wolf. It is not courage of a warrior that makes one worthy, rather courage of the heart. You must first drive out the demon of resentment from your soul, and then forgive your brother for any injustice you think he has caused you. And you must forgive the white man as well, as I have forgiven those who have put me here in this tree of torment. Only then will you have proven yourself to the Great Spirit. And only then will He deem you worthy to be counted amongst his warriors of the eternal sun."

Lone Wolf was deeply troubled. Forgive his brother? And, now, forgive the white man—after all he and his people had suffered? How could the Spirit ask this of him?

"Heed my words, Lone Wolf, before it is too late. Purge the demons of resentment and hatred from your soul, so that the Great Spirit may dwell there, as he does atop the sacred cliffs."

The Spirit spoke one last time, "Whoever hears my word, hears the Great Spirit."

Was it the Great Spirit himself, Lone Wolf wondered, who was now putting him to the test, while there before him was the Spirit of The Word, sent to challenge him as never before.

Looking back to the site of the village, Lone Wolf thought of his brother, Rising Bear. Was it possible he was still alive after thirty snows? If he were, where had he been during all that time? How could he have avoided the white settlers who had occupied their land? And where could he be now, or where could his weathered bones be found?

Turning around, Lone Wolf again looked up into the tree. The Spirit had vanished. Stillness settled over the forest.

During the night and all the following day, Lone Wolf made camp at the base of the tree, hoping the Spirit would reappear. But only His words remained, words that Lone Wolf had not wanted to hear. What must he do, he asked himself, to battle the demons of resentment and hatred that had long dwelt within his soul, demons that now had to be conquered before he could ever cross over to the Spirit Land.

Lone Wolf made his way back to the ridge-of-the-three-pines that overlooked the river. As he prayed, the words of the Spirit returned to haunt him.

Forgive his brother? Forgive the white man? How could he, after all they had done to him?

A gentle breeze began to blow across the Mahikanittuc from the sacred cliffs on the far shore. One day, Lone Wolf knew, he must stand there before the

Great Spirit, to give an account of his life. For the sacred cliffs were the gateway to the Spirit Land.

Then once again he heard the call of distant drums.

Chapter 15

Brothers-of-the-Same-Birth

Was it possible Rising Bear was still alive, Lone Wolf wondered, as he made his way through the empty forest. How could his brother have survived here in their ancestral lands during all that time, in a place long since occupied by the white man?

Rising Bear, for certain, must have been killed by the Dutch at the time of the attack on the village. Even if he had escaped, he would surely have fled long ago to some distant land, perhaps like Lone Wolf, living among an adopted tribe. As a fugitive, who knew where he might be?

But the Spirit in the tree had put Lone Wolf to the test. He must seek out his brother, and make his peace with him, once and for all, or with his weathered bones. If Rising Bear were already dead, what chance did Lone Wolf have of finding any trace of him? The animals of the woods, by this time, would have carried off his weathered bones to where only the Great Spirit now knew their resting place.

Why should he search for his brother at all? It was Rising Bear who should seek out Lone Wolf's forgiveness instead. Had he not competed against Lone Wolf to succeed their father as Warrior Chief? Being of the same birth either one, by custom, was entitled to lead their people in battle. It was the fault of Rising Bear that their father had delayed bestowing this honor on one of his sons, until it was too late. Lone Wolf had never forgiven Rising Bear for that.

As the days passed, Lone Wolf began to feel regret. How foolish to have returned here at all to his native land. His people were all gone...dead or banished.

What was the purpose, if the Great Spirit who dwelt on the sacred cliffs would not command his father's spirit to reveal the words he had taken to his grave? Lone Wolf had traveled a great distance, overcoming many hardships, only to live out his remaining days alone, secluded in the woods, forever wary of the whites. He was now an outcast in his own land, left behind by the passage of time.

Returning again to the sacred tree, he camped there for the night. Perhaps the Spirit of The Word would reappear and help him seek out his father one last time. But there was only the silence of the empty forest.

Sadness overcame Lone Wolf's spirit. His life now seemed without purpose. Why had he left the Northern Plains, and the freedom he had known there to roam the endless horizons? He should have stayed to live out his remaining days as Warrior Chief of his adopted people, the fierce Blackfoot-Blood, who still ruled over their ancestral lands. But something had lured him back from that distant land. Now that he had finally returned, there was nothing here for him, neither the Great Spirit nor the spirit of his father, not even the companionship of any mortal, only the haunting words of the Spirit in the tree, words that further burdened his soul.

Lone Wolf fell into a deep sleep. In his dreams he saw the enchanted woods of his ancestral lands, the secluded places within the forest that he had known since a boy, places now empty, without trace of his vanquished people—only his lone figure, forever searching.

***

Game had become scarce as white settlers continued to cut deeper into the forest to make room for their farms. Lone Wolf traveled farther north beyond the Pocantico River, near the land of the Sint Sink, to find prey.

Returning from a hunt, he followed the northern branch of Wysquaqua Creek from its origin where it flowed out of weathered rock. On his back he carried a deer, felled by a single arrow. He would smoke its meat and store it for the winter ahead.

When he neared where both branches of the stream join as one, there came the sound of drums. They were the drums he had heard, from time to time, throughout his life on the Northern Plains.

Lone Wolf dropped the deer and broke into a run. He followed the streambed back toward the site of the village. As he passed through the limestone gorge, the drums grew louder.

He hurried along the stream, slipping at times off the wet rocks. When a short distance from where the Wysquaqua flows into the Mahikanittuc, the drums fell silent.

Had he imagined it? No, what he had heard was real! He would find its source, no matter how long the search.

Lone Wolf made camp for the night, close to the river. He waited. The forest was soon covered in darkness. He would resume his search in the morning.

No sooner had he lain down than the drums began again. He listened closely. They were from the north, from farther upriver.

As the clouds cleared, a full moon illuminated the forest. Lone Wolf again made his way toward the drums. He stopped for a moment to get a bearing on their elusive source. Again, they fell silent.

Sitting down on a fallen tree, Lone Wolf waited. There was no doubt now. The drums were like those he had first heard as a child. There was someone in these woods besides himself...one of his own tribe!

The drums began again. Lone Wolf sprang to his feet, then charged into the woods like a wounded bear. As he tore through the underbrush, the drums grew louder still.

He reached a narrow ridge, barely wide enough to stand on. The ridge ran a short distance, then disappeared. He could go no farther.

The place seemed familiar. He had been here before. The moonlight revealed a steep embankment below the ridge, and the Mahikanittuc just beyond.

The memories returned. It was on this ridge that he had once entered a cave, for the test of courage to become a warrior. But where was the cave? Where was its opening? As he searched, he found it had become overgrown by heavy brush. One would never have known there was a cave here at all.

From within the shrubs that covered the opening came the sound of drums, louder than ever. Who could be in the cave at this time of night, beating on drums?

Cutting the overgrowth with his stone knife, Lone Wolf worked his way through the opening, careful not to make noise.

He walked slowly into the dark cavern, holding his knife at the ready. The drums echoed from the back reaches of the cave then fell silent again. As he rounded a bend in the passage, he saw the glow of a campfire.

Seated beside the fire, his back turned, was an old man with long gray hair. He was praying quietly. Reaching down the old man picked up a wooden flute from which came haunting, melodic tones that resonated throughout the depths of the cave. Then, again, he beat the drum.

Lone Wolf stood motionless. There was no doubt. He had heard this very same drum from time to time throughout his life, far in the land of the Blackfoot. How could this be?

The old, gray-haired man, unaware someone was behind him, began to chant aloud. Lone Wolf recognized the words immediately. They were of the Algonquin tongue, the Munsee Dialect, the language of his own people. The prayers were those of a medicine man, used in healing ceremonies.

The old man, still unaware he was being watched, went about mixing herbs in a stone bowl. Staring into the fire, he chanted special prayers to the spirits.

The musty air caused Lone Wolf to sneeze. The old man struggled to get to his feet. He turned toward the intruder. "Who goes there?" he asked in a nervous voice.

Lone Wolf looked closely at the stranger as glows from the campfire now illuminated the old, wrinkled face. There was no doubt, despite the passage of time. The old man's features resembled his own, like a brother-of-the-same-birth.

"Rising Bear!" Lone Wolf called to him, though they stood only a short distance apart.

"What manner of being are you," Rising Bear asked, "that you come here in the darkness of night, find my hidden refuge, and call me by name?"

Lone Wolf realized his brother's eyesight must be failing, as he watched him squint his eyes then peer intently.

"Are you the Spirit of Death," Rising Bear asked in a trembling voice? "Have you finally come to take me away?"

"No, Rising Bear! It is I, Lone Wolf! Your own brother, Lone Wolf! Do you not recognize me? I have finally returned."

"Lone Wolf!" Rising Bear said. "Is it truly you, after all this time? I feared you had met your end long ago, though I have always prayed for your return. Welcome back, Brother, to our ancestral lands."

"I thought you, too, Rising Bear, had long since met your death," Lone Wolf said. "That you had fallen at the time of the attack on our village."

Rising Bear stepped closer to where the light of the campfire was brighter. He stretched out his arm in welcome.

Lone Wolf hesitated, then finally extended his own.

The brothers-of-the-same-birth sat down around the campfire. Rising Bear added more wood to see each other in better light. He brought out food, a tart mixture of ground acorns and wild berries.

"Tell me, Brother," Lone Wolf asked, "how is it that you were not killed nor taken captive by the Dutch?"

"During the surprise attack on our village," Rising Bear began his story, "I was shot in the head. But the musket ball glanced off, knocking me to the ground where I lay senseless well into the night.

"The white soldiers, seeing blood covering my head and face, thought I was dead. When I regained my wits later that night, I found myself lying amongst a pile of bodies — men, women and children of our tribe, massacred and dumped into an open grave. Under cover of dark, I worked my way free of the tangled, charred bodies, then ran off into the woods. I watched from a distance as the remnants of our people and yourself, Lone Wolf, were led off by the horse soldiers the following day."

"For one moon," Rising Bear continued, "I remained hidden deep within the forest where the white man seldom ventures. Unable to hunt in the open for fear of being seen, I kept alive by foraging for roots and berries, always at night.

"As the weather became colder, I searched for better shelter. It was then that I came to this cave. Lying along a narrow ridge and facing the river, it is difficult for anyone to see or to gain access to. With the passage of time the shrubs have grown thicker around the opening, as you saw, hiding it completely."

"Have you lived in this cave during all that time?" Lone Wolf asked his brother in disbelief.

"Yes, Lone Wolf, I have lived here ever since, hoping some day you would return, together with our banished tribe, so that we might reclaim our land. Each day since, I have beaten the sacred drum, praying for the wind to carry its sound to you, the drums of your people calling you home."

"Indeed I have heard them," Lone Wolf said. "Far in the lands of the Blackfoot where I lived all that time."

"So I had hoped that with your return," Rising Bear continued, "our ancestral lands could once again be ours, and our people could live as we did since the long ago. But as time passed, I realized this never again could be."

"How so?" Lone Wolf asked.

"The white settlers have increased in numbers. They continue to land on our shores in their ships of tall sails, an endless stream of invaders. Once here they multiply like rabbits, having many children to help work their farms."

"Ha," Lone Wolf laughed. "Like rabbits!"

"With more of their kind," Rising Bear went on, "they cut down trees to make room for their farms. As the forest has become smaller with time, much of the game has disappeared. Few of the animals we once knew, when we were children, remain in these woods. The beaver, the bear and your namesake, the wolf, are long since gone. Even the deer are now few."

"This I have seen for myself, Rising Bear, much to my distress."

"The land, Lone Wolf, is no longer as when our people dwelt within this forest, and held it in reverence as the Great Spirit's creation." There was sadness in Rising Bear's voice.

"The white man has no respect for the land," Lone Wolf said. "In his greed he destroys all that is good."

"But tell me, Lone Wolf," Rising Bear said. "What has happened to you since you left the Mahikanittuc long ago? What did the horse soldiers do with you, and with our people, after burning our village and leading you off? And what has become of our mother?"

Lone Wolf recounted the story of the forced march. He told of the bitter cold their people had to endure along the journey, and the death of their mother, left behind, buried in snow. He described the resettlement of the Weckquasgeek on the reservation and his own escape from the fort. Then of his wandering into the Northern Plains to settle among the Blackfoot. And finally his sad visit to the reservation during his return journey.

"Disease and rum have decimated what remained of our people," Lone Wolf lamented. "They have no hunting grounds from which to take game to feed their families. No longer able to hunt, they line up like beggars, for food and blankets brought in by wagon. Their numbers have dwindled to only a few, as the white man's diseases bring them plague after plague. Our people, as we once knew them, are no more. You and I, Rising Bear, will soon be the last of our kind."

The two brothers sat in silence. They ate the remaining acorns and berries.

"These people you call the Blackfoot, tell me, Lone Wolf, what was your life like amongst them? Are they hunters and warriors? Did they accept you as one of their own?"

"They did accept me as their own," Lone Wolf answered, "after I had first proven myself. They are great hunters and warriors, known to other tribes as 'masters of the Northern Plains.' Their fierceness and bravery has no equal. It is strange, Rising Bear, for they speak an ancient form of Algonquin, much like our own tongue. Perhaps in the past, we were one people."

Lone Wolf went on well into the night to recount his life amongst the Blackfoot. He told his brother of all that had happened to him: being adopted by the tribe; becoming Warrior Chief; marrying Spring Woman; burying his only son, Swift Elk, after he had been killed hunting the Great Buffalo, and of his own encounter with the creature.

Rising Bear listened intently to his brother's stories. He was fascinated by Lone Wolf's adventures during the more than thirty snows since leaving the Eastern Woodlands. It was in marked contrast to his own life, Rising Bear thought. He had lived as a hermit, hidden in this refuge of a cave, without family or tribe. For in truth he had been like his own banished people, a captive of the white man, no longer free to roam.

Their thoughts returned to the present, as Rising Bear added more wood to the fire.

"When I entered the cave," Lone Wolf said, noticing the stone bowl once again, "I saw you making medicine. Do you still practice the ancient customs of our people?"

"Yes, Lone Wolf, I follow the medicine way. I make the special cures, handed down from our ancestors, using plants to heal both body and spirit. But as I have become older, my memory fails from time to time, and certain cures I no longer recall. It is difficult, for without one's people to treat, I cannot practice as a medicine man is accustomed."

"What medicine were you preparing when I entered the cave?"

Rising Bear reached for the stone bowl nearby and showed it to Lone Wolf.

"These are from the yellow petals of the starflower. It grows only along the edge of Wysquaqua Creek. I use this for the sharp pain I feel at times within my chest. It is a powerful cure, but as of late I have had difficulty finding much of this flowering plant. There is precious little of it left in our land, though, like our people, it once flourished throughout."

"Do you search for these plants during the day?" Lone Wolf asked.

"I venture out mostly at night so as not to be seen by the white settlers. That is why I have been able to survive here as long as I have, and to go undetected."

"I take different medicines in addition to this," Rising Bear went on further to explain, pointing to various stone bowls alongside the fire, each with its special cure.

"Without these, Lone Wolf, I would have been here to greet you only as a skeleton. I am a sick man. The dampness of the cave and my hidden way of life have weakened my body, though not my spirit. I fear my days are now few."

There was silence for a moment.

"But then," Rising Bear continued, "I am ready to leave this world, for I yearn to see once again our mother, and our father, and all the people of the past with whom we had once shared a happier life."

At the mention of his father, Lone Wolf's face tightened. Resentment toward his brother rekindled in his heart.

"But I give thanks to the Great Spirit," Rising Bear continued, "that He has allowed me to live long enough to see you return, before my time has come to cross over to the Spirit Land."

Lone Wolf did not answer. The words of the Spirit in the tree unexpectedly returned to mind, "Seek out and forgive your brother." But how could he, after what Rising Bear had done to him?

"Do you have fresh meat in the cave?" Lone Wolf asked.

"No, Lone Wolf, I have not eaten fresh meat for the longest time. I snatch a squirrel or woodchuck that might wander by the cave from time to time, but no large game. It has gotten too difficult to hunt at night as I did when my eyes were better and the game not as scarce. How I wish I could taste roasted deer once again."

"Then I shall hunt."

Lone Wolf suddenly stood up then left abruptly, in the middle of the night. Rising Bear, still seated, watched in shock as his brother walked out of the cave without another word.

In his heart, Lone Wolf was more troubled than ever.

151

Chapter 16

Warrior Chief

The water flowing out of the fissured rock was as cold as when Lone Wolf first drank from it as a boy. Cupping his hands, he drew the refreshing water to his lips. How timeless was this spring, Lone Wolf thought. It had flowed since the long ago, generations of Weckquasgeek drinking its waters. One day, he would be the last.

His thoughts returned to Rising Bear. He remembered how they had been fierce rivals while growing up. Even here at this spring, he would race Rising Bear through the woods, to see who would drink from these waters first. He still felt resentment — but now also sorrow for his brother's ill health and for the lonely, secluded life he had led. Lone Wolf had lived amongst the Blackfoot, free to roam the Northern Plains, far from the white man. During all that time Rising Bear had lived alone, in hiding.

But was it not Rising Bear, Lone Wolf reminded himself, who had competed against him to succeed their father as Warrior Chief...until the very last when their father met an unexpected death. Because of his brother, Lone Wolf was never to know what was in his father's heart. And now the Great Spirit would not send him the vision he had sought throughout his life, a vision of his father, speaking the words he had taken to his grave.

Lone Wolf had promised to bring fresh meat back to his brother. He would keep his word. But then he would be done with him.

Returning to Wysquaqua Creek, Lone Wolf found the deer from his kill of the previous day. The scavengers had not gotten to it. With his prey draped over his shoulders, he made his way back to Rising Bear's cave.

He thought for a moment of confronting his brother about his feelings, but felt uneasy on how to raise the matter.

He reached the cave and, with the deer still on his back, forced his way through the shrubs that covered the opening. Inside he found Rising Bear sound asleep in a midday nap. His snoring echoed from the back reaches of the cave. Lone Wolf placed the deer by the campfire, then left quietly without waking his brother. He had kept his word. There was no need to ever return.

It would be best, he thought, to leave this area forever. There was nothing left to keep him here. He would travel north, beyond the Pocantico, where the forests had not been cut, and there was game left to hunt.

Lone Wolf made his way upstream, along the northern branch of the Wysquaqua. Once again, he was leaving his ancestral lands, he thought, but this time never to return. He would travel north, far from the white man. Perhaps he would find there another tribe among which to live. Then again, perhaps he would return to the Northern Plains to live out his life with Bird Rattler and the Blackfoot.

At the northernmost reach of Wysquaqua Creek, he noticed a cluster of yellow starflowers growing along the edge of the stream. He remembered these were the plants used by his brother to make the medicine that relieved the pain in his chest, plants that had become difficult to find.

Staring down at the flowers, Lone Wolf again recalled the words of the Spirit in the tree, "You must seek out your brother, and make your peace with him, once and for all."

Lone Wolf pulled all the starflower plants out of the ground, roots and all. He made his way back downstream, returning to the hidden cave. He would bring Rising Bear the plants needed for the medicine that kept him alive. He would also confront him, once and for all, with the seething resentment that had long afflicted his heart.

***

After entering the cave, a strange fear came over Lone Wolf. Would he be able to reveal his feelings to Rising Bear, feelings that bordered on jealousy and hatred of his own brother?

Rising Bear had already awakened, and was about to finish roasting the deer meat.

"I was surprised when I awoke to see it lying there," Rising Bear said. "Thank you, Lone Wolf, for the deer you brought. We shall eat well now. I have prepared it the way you like, done to a crisp brown."

Lone Wolf handed the star flowers, roots and all, to his brother.

Rising Bear's eyes lit up. "I must thank you once again, Lone Wolf, for your thoughtfulness. With these flowers I will make my special medicine, since very little remains. You have brought the plants that will allow me to see the sun rise yet again."

"Take the plants," Lone Wolf said, "and place their roots into the earth so you may grow them as you need. See here, the roots are intact."

"Indeed, Lone Wolf, this will make it easier for me. How wise. Again, my gratitude to you for all you have done."

How could Lone Wolf confront him now? With his thankful words, Rising Bear had made it more difficult than ever. And how could he confront a brother who had lived such a solitary life, and who had prayed unceasingly for his return?

The two brothers sat down around the fire and ate the roasted deer meat. Lone Wolf did not speak. A cold silence hung in the air like a mist that would not lift.

How could he ever make peace with his brother, Lone Wolf asked himself again, if he did not first vent all

154

his feelings, no matter how bitter they might be? But it had become more difficult now, as Lone Wolf felt growing pity for a brother whose health had suffered greatly from his long captivity within the cave. And even more pity for the lonely life he had led, without human companionship, without wife or child. Perhaps, then, it was better that such feelings remained unspoken.

As they sat there eating, Rising Bear kept staring into his brother's distressed eyes.

"Speak to me, Lone Wolf. There is something that troubles you deeply. Your silence speaks louder than words."

That was the opportunity he had waited for. Lone Wolf put down the roasted meat he was eating.

"Yes, Rising Bear, since you ask, there are feelings I have carried within my heart for the longest time, feelings known only to the Great Spirit."

"Then, Lone Wolf," Rising Bear reassured him in a gentle voice, "please speak freely and unburden your heart. We are brothers-of-the-same-birth and should share openly our true feelings, be they good or bad— while we still have time."

With that encouragement, Lone Wolf allowed his emotions to finally erupt.

"You always knew, Brother, that I wanted more than anything in life to succeed our father as Warrior Chief. Yet, throughout our youth, you challenged me in everything we did. You competed against me, relentlessly, to win our father's favor, and to gain for yourself his coveted headdress of Warrior Chief. Each time I would prevail. But you persisted in your challenges, forever putting me to the test.

"You knew as surely as we sit here," Lone Wolf went on, with anger in his voice, "that I had proven myself among all the warriors of our tribe, yourself included. Yet, you continued to compete against me, and thus deny me what was rightfully mine, until it was too late.

155

"Throughout my life," Lone Wolf's voice now saddened, "I have carried this burden in my heart, of not knowing what my father thought of me. Did he deem me worthy to succeed him?"

Rising Bear's eyes grew more pensive as he continued to listen.

"And so, ever since becoming a warrior," Lone Wolf now finished, "I have strived to prove my courage among all who have challenged me, mortals and spirits alike. I have cowered before none! I have proven myself to all...to all except our father."

The two brothers sat quietly around the fire. The flames illuminated their wrinkled faces, mirroring the hardships each had endured throughout his life.

Rising Bear finally broke the silence.

"My Brother," he said in a gentle voice, "it is now time for me to speak openly, and to unburden my own heart of the feelings that have lain hidden for so long."

Lone Wolf looked into Rising Bear's face and saw his eyes beginning to mist. Rising Bear cleared his throat, then spoke again.

"I never wanted to become Warrior Chief of our people, never! I wished only to be a medicine man, a healer, like those of old, gathering the plants the Great Spirit has given us and releasing their special powers to restore health to our people. I am a simple man, Lone Wolf, one who loves the things of nature and the medicine way. That was all I ever wanted to be, not a Warrior Chief."

"Why then did you compete against me, Rising Bear, always challenging me?" Lone Wolf asked.

"Such was the wish of our father. I could not tell you at the time, but since he is long dead, my oath to him no longer serves its purpose. There was no opportunity to tell you before, for when our village was burned, we were separated."

"I do not understand. What oath do you speak of?"

"Our father made me swear an oath," Rising Bear answered, his voice breaking with emotion. "An oath, Lone Wolf, I did not want to take: to challenge you at every chance; to make you strive harder; to toughen you for battle so that none would ever be your equal."

"But why, Rising Bear? Why did my father, and you, do this to me?"

"There was never any doubt in our father's mind," Rising Bear went on, "never any doubt at all that you were deserving. He had wanted you alone to succeed him, and to become the greatest Warrior Chief our people had ever known. As his successor, you were to have been the fiercest of warriors, feared by every white man who ever heard your name."

Lone Wolf sat quietly for a while. He finally spoke. "What made my father so relentless in his demands on me, Rising Bear? Why was it that no matter what challenge I would overcome, I could never satisfy him? And why could I never win his praise?"

"Our father hoped to drive the white man from our lands forever," Rising Bear answered. "For he made a grave mistake, which I once overheard him tell our mother. He had placed his mark on a written treaty with the Dutch. It was said, at the time, this was necessary to confirm the 'spoken-words treaty' agreed to by our grandfather long before, which gave the white man shared rights to our hunting grounds. Without this written treaty, the English, new to our shores, would not have recognized the prior land claims of the Dutch. This grave mistake our father came to regret deeply, and it burdened his heart ever more as the number of white settlers grew steadily.

"With his own mark placed on the treaty," Rising Bear continued, "he could no longer take up arms against the white settlers and so violate his sworn word. As for you, Lone Wolf, you were free to do otherwise. You were to have been his successor, the fiercest of Warrior Chiefs, driving the white man back into the waters from which he had come. You were to undo the mistakes of our father, and of our grandfather before him, by reclaiming our ancestral lands they had unwittingly ceded to the white man. And so our father placed all his hopes in you, that you would restore his honor, as he could no longer do himself."

"I never knew!" Lone Wolf said. "I was unaware that our father harbored such feelings of regret for his own mistake in signing a treaty. I knew of his resentment toward the ever-growing number of white settlers, but never of the guilt he felt for the loss of our tribal lands."

"And so, Lone Wolf, I swore the oath he asked of me," Rising Bear went on, his eyes beginning to tear. "It was an oath I pleaded with him not to take. But I was told it was my duty as a son to help our father in his purpose of putting you to the test, so that you would strive ever harder and grow in skill and courage. There was never any doubt in his mind, Lone Wolf. You had proven yourself to our father, and won his admiration. It was you who was to have succeeded him. It was you who was to drive the white man from our lands, in his stead."

As Rising Bear revealed the truth that had lain hidden from him all of his life, Lone Wolf felt a deep sense of peace.

"I am sorry, Lone Wolf, truly sorry, for causing you such distress. I never wanted to be Chief, but our father made me take this oath, from which he would not release me. We must understand, and forgive him. It was his way of dealing with the guilt he carried within."

There was silence in the cave. Lone Wolf stood up, then gave a supporting arm to Rising Bear as he struggled to get to his feet.

"I deeply regret, Brother," Rising Bear said, "the anguish I have caused you over these many snows."

"You have lifted a great burden from my heart," Lone Wolf said, a tear flowing down his face. He embraced his brother. "Forgive me, Rising Bear, for the resentment I have harbored against you all this time. Forgive me."

Rising Bear embraced Lone Wolf, in turn. The two brothers stood a while, then sat down again.

After adding more wood to the fire, Rising Bear turned toward his brother.

"Is there something else, Lone Wolf, that remains unsaid?"

"You are truly wise, Brother, in matters of the spirit." Lone Wolf hesitated for a moment before speaking again. "There is one other thing . . . why did our father never show his feelings towards us as we grew older?"

Rising Bear understood the burden remaining in his brother's heart.

"Our father cared for us both, Lone Wolf. But as we grew into boyhood, he found it difficult to show his love openly. It was not his way, for he was, in truth, a modest man. Perhaps, too, he might have thought he would weaken the fierceness he struggled so hard to nurture in you. But I heard him express to our mother, at times when you were not present, the deep love he had always felt for you since you were a child."

Once again a tear flowed down Lone Wolf's face. He now realized that these were also words that he had always wanted to hear. He understood what the Spirit of The Word had meant: "Forgive your brother, and you will know inner peace as never before."

"I am grateful, Rising Bear," Lone Wolf said in a choking voice. "I am grateful, good brother, for unburdening my heart, and for your having waited here for my return during all that time. Let us now eat this roasted meat and have our fill. It will restore strength to our bodies, as you have restored my spirit!"

The two brothers feasted well into the afternoon, recalling happier times they had shared together as children growing up. The memories all came back, of hunting, fishing, canoeing on the Mahikanittuc, and of the tricks they enjoyed playing on the elders of the tribe who had trouble telling the brothers apart.

The memories seemed to rush back, as vivid as when they had first happened, of summers long past when the forests belonged to the Weckquasgeek alone, and the drums of their people could be heard throughout the land.

* * *

It was late in the day when the two brothers finished their storytelling. Rising Bear asked Lone Wolf to meet him at the site where their village had once stood. Lone Wolf, though bewildered, went ahead. He waited patiently for his brother to appear, not knowing what to expect.

Rising Bear finally came into view, carrying a small bundle under his arm.

"Come here, Lone Wolf," his brother said, "beneath the sacred cedar. Stand on this flat stone, 'the stone of Chiefs.'"

Lone Wolf needed no reminding. He recalled his father Gray Eagle standing on this very stone whenever he addressed the tribe. The stone, covered with specks of silver mica, had been left there in the long ago when the great ice receded from the valley.

Lone Wolf followed his brother's instructions without question, stepping onto the raised stone. With his back toward the river, he faced what had once been the center of their village.

Was Rising Bear's mind failing him, Lone Wolf wondered, as they both stood there a while.

Rising Bear finally took the bundle from under his arm and removed a headdress made of eagle feathers, trimmed in wolf fur. It was the headdress of Warrior Chief, passed down by generations of Weckquasgeek, and last worn by their father.

"Shortly before our village was attacked," Rising Bear began, as though addressing the tribe, "our father confided in me that you, Lone Wolf, would soon succeed him as Warrior Chief. He also confided that he would personally bestow upon you this sacred headdress, as he had longed to do. But with the winds of change blowing fiercely through our lands, he was prevented from fulfilling his wish."

"You have saved the best for last!" Lone Wolf said.

"Lone Wolf, I now stand in his place," Rising Bear continued. "On behalf of our father, and in his name, I bestow upon you the headdress he once wore. In the words he would have spoken, 'you have earned this honor by virtue of your great skills as a hunter and unfailing courage as a warrior.'"

"These are words I had longed to hear," Lone Wolf said, his voice now breaking.

Rising Bear placed the war bonnet on Lone Wolf's head then, stepping back, declared, "Until the Great Spirit finally calls you from this world, you are the Warrior Chief of the Weckquasgeek."

Raising his arm, Rising Bear acknowledged the new Chief with a tribal war cry. He then left to return to the cave, leaving his brother by himself.

Lone Wolf stood a while, atop the stone of Chiefs. The sun, setting above the cliffs behind him, silhouetted his figure in a halo of crimson and gold.

He looked out onto the open area, once the center of the village which, for a ceremony such as this, would have been filled with all his people. They would have taken part in a special tribute and in the celebration and feasting that would have followed.

As his mind began to wander, he saw the ghosts of his people, walking slowly out of the shadows of the surrounding forest. There too, the last to come into view, was the spirit of his father, watching from a distance. He had returned!

161

Warriors of his tribe were dressed for the ceremonial Eagle Dance. Long feathers covered their shoulders and arms so as to resemble wings. On the back of each was a cluster of tail feathers. The warriors began to dance, circling about with outstretched arms, like a bird in flight, turning its wings into the wind. They were calling upon the eagle, most sacred of birds, that they too would soar in spirit, and remain forever free.

Lone Wolf, standing on the stone of Chiefs, watched in awe. Then, one by one, his people returned to the forest, disappearing into the shadows. His father's spirit was the last to leave. They had come back, if only for a fleeting moment.

"How unfair is life!" Lone Wolf spoke aloud, as though addressing his tribe. "After all this time, after all the battles I have fought, I have realized my boyhood dream, to win the praise of my father and to wear his coveted headdress.

"At long last," Lone Wolf cried out to the towering oaks that surrounded the village. "I am the Warrior Chief of the Weckquasgeek—the Chief of a people who are no more!"

His words, like the rays of the setting sun, faded into the depths of the empty forest.

Chapter 17

Crossing to the Spirit Land

Lone Wolf sat by the fire and watched as Rising Bear mixed roots and herbs for another of his medicine cures. How sad it would be, he thought, for one day all this knowledge, handed down from their ancestors since the long ago, would be lost forever. None of their tribe remained to pass on the acquired wisdom of the medicine way. It would disappear with Rising Bear and, like their people, forgotten for all time.

The roasted deer meat was gone. Lone Wolf finished sharpening his spear point. "I will hunt, Rising Bear, and return later in the day."

"Before you leave, Lone Wolf, I have this special medicine for you. It is one I use myself from time to time."

"What is this medicine for, Rising Bear? My bones ache when it rains, but other than that I am not ill."

"You complained, Lone Wolf, that your eyes have begun to fail you, your vision becoming blurred at times. I have taken roots and pollen of the ista plant, mixing them with deer fat, to make this special medicine that will restore your sight."

Rising Bear proceeded to apply the fragrant ointment onto Lone Wolf's eyelids, his fingers moving in a circular pattern. He chanted a prayer, imploring the healing spirits locked deep within the plant to release their power.

Lone Wolf blinked his eyes a few times, then looked around the cave. In moments the mixture began its magical cure.

"Brother," Lone Wolf said, "your skills as a medicine man are beyond belief. Already my vision is clear, and my eyes are once again in sharp focus, as when I was a boy. Now I see clearly...and in more ways than one."

Rising Bear smiled.

Lone Wolf left the cave, more determined than ever to bring back a large buck to feast upon, in appreciation of his brother's cures—both of body and of spirit.

***

There are days on the hunt, Lone Wolf thought, when no game can be found, no matter how hard one searches. Then there are days like today, when it seems all the animals of the woods have come out into the open, as though offering themselves to be taken.

Lone Wolf spotted several deer feeding in tall brush on the side of a hill. Within moments he targeted a large buck, its huge rack of antlers towering above the others. The hunt was over as quickly as it had begun.

The slain animal was heavy, giving him trouble as he struggled to lift it to his shoulders. Carrying it back to the cave, Lone Wolf stopped along the way to unload his prey and rest. He recalled that as a young warrior he could easily have carried such heavy game through the woods. Much of the strength he had relied upon throughout his life seemed to have been sapped from him during his long journey home, like the salmon in Bird Rattler's vision. But he was still able to hunt, and now, with Rising Bear's special medicine, his eyesight had been restored.

At last, the cave was near. Lone Wolf rested once more, making certain he could not be seen. He fell asleep, then was awakened by the cries of scavenging crows that had descended upon his game. With one sweep of his spear, he sent them into frenzied flight.

Picking up the heavy carcass, he slung it over his shoulders again and continued on his way. The cave came into view.

Lone Wolf froze in his tracks. Could it be the medicine Rising Bear had placed on his eyes was making

164

him see things? As he approached the cave, he saw a white man forcing his way through the shrubs that hid the opening.

His worst fear had come true. Rising Bear's hiding place had finally been discovered. His brother was in danger of being taken captive!

Lone Wolf dropped the deer, then ran toward the cave. He tore through the shrubs that covered the opening.

Rising Bear was sitting alone at the rear of the cave, preoccupied in the preparation of yet another medicine. As the white man approached his brother, Lone Wolf charged from behind. Leaping onto the back of the intruder, Lone Wolf wrapped both arms tightly around his neck. The intruder gasped for breath. Pulling out a stone knife, Lone Wolf pressed the sharp edge against his throat.

The white man, a youth of sixteen or so, gave out a loud cry.

"Help me, Rising Bear! Help me, please!"

"Lone Wolf, do not harm him! He is a friend. I know him. He is a friend."

"A friend?" Lone Wolf said in disbelief, his arms still wrapped tightly around him. "A white man is your friend?"

"Yes, a friend. He visits me from time to time. He brings food, and plants for my medicines."

"Why did you not tell me before?" Lone Wolf asked.

"I had meant to," Rising Bear answered, "when the time was right."

Lone Wolf stood motionless for a moment, then releasing his grip, threw the intruder down to the ground. He walked out of the cave without another word.

For the remainder of the morning Lone Wolf waited outside. He would not reenter the cave while the white youth was still there. At midday the intruder finally came out, cautiously looking around. When he caught sight of Lone Wolf standing near his deer, he made a break for the woods.

Lone Wolf reentered the cave, carrying the large buck over his shoulders. He dropped it alongside the campfire where his brother was still seated.

"I do not understand, Rising Bear," Lone Wolf began immediately. "How could you befriend a white! Does your mind fail you? He is one of those who killed our people, and who stole all that had been ours. How could one from such a treacherous race ever be called a 'friend'?"

"This boy, himself, did none of the things you speak of," Rising Bear said. "He discovered my hiding place by accident over two snows ago while hunting a rabbit. He has never told anyone. His word is good."

"Good? The word of the white man can never be good!" Lone Wolf shouted. "Have you forgotten their betrayals, and the evils they have inflicted upon our people? The broken treaties and theft of our lands? Have you forgotten the surprise attack on our village, the slaughter of our women and children trapped in burning lodges? And the death of our father, long before his time?"

"I remember, Lone Wolf. I remember only too well, all that we suffered at the hands of the white man, from his greed and treachery. But this boy is innocent of these acts. One cannot blame a son for the sins of his father."

Lone Wolf grunted in disgust.

"He is a good person, with a loving heart," Rising Bear pleaded. "He has been my only friend since I went into hiding in this lonely refuge."

Lone Wolf's face remained frozen.

"Do you know what it is like, Brother," Rising Bear continued, "to be truly lonely, living by oneself during all that time since you left our land, hiding in a cave, keeping out of sight of people, without anyone with whom to speak nor to share your feelings and thoughts?

There is a loneliness in this life that one can never know, unless he has lived it. The heart becomes very heavy indeed, without the warmth of human companionship."

Rising Bear paused for a moment, then drank from a clay jar containing his starflower medicine. Seeing that Lone Wolf was still unmoved, he saved his sharpest arrow for last.

"I was not free to roam the plains, as you were, Lone Wolf. You had a tribe, an adopted people to call your own. You had a wife and son. I had no one, only this boy to call my friend. A white boy, yes, but one whose goodness and loyalty can never be questioned."

After hearing Rising Bear's final plea, Lone Wolf bowed his head. He felt sorrow for his brother, for the lonely life he had led, waiting for his return.

"If you choose to call him friend, then I will question you no more. But as for me, he will always be one of them."

It was Rising Bear's turn to grunt.

"How does he call himself?" Lone Wolf asked.

"David Philipse. But I call him 'Philipse'."

"Does his father not question him when he comes to the cave?"

"He has neither father nor mother," Rising Bear answered. "He was orphaned as a child. Both parents were burned to death with the rest of his brothers and sisters when their house of wood caught fire. He has been raised ever since by his uncle, one called 'Jacobs,' a brutal man who works him hard on the farm that lies south of Wysquaqua Creek."

"Can you trust him not to give away your hiding place?" Lone Wolf asked.

"For over two snows he has proven himself to be as loyal a friend as one could have. Judge him for what he is and, I assure you, you will find no fault."

Later that day, after Rising Bear had finished roasting the buck from Lone Wolf's hunt, the two brothers sat down to feast again.

As they began to eat, they heard a noise at the entrance of the cave. Someone was forcing his way through the shrubs that covered the opening. Lone Wolf jumped to his feet and pulled out his stone knife. Young Philipse appeared from out of the bend in the tunnel. To Lone Wolf's surprise, he had returned. He was afraid to come any closer. Lone Wolf, at Rising Bear's request, finally put away his knife and sat down.

Rising Bear motioned with his hand for Philipse to join him alongside the fire. He approached cautiously, then sat as far as he could from Lone Wolf. Glows from the campfire reflected off the youth's blond hair and pale skin, in sharp contrast to the two swarthy-skinned Weckquasgeek.

The boy sat quietly, fidgeting his fingers.

Rising Bear tore off a large piece of roasted meat and handed it to Philipse.

No sooner had the youth opened his mouth to take his first bite, than Lone Wolf snatched the meat out of his hands and threw it to the ground.

"It is my meat, from my kill," he shouted at Philipse.

Philipse's face turned red with shame.

Rising Bear dropped his eyes. Sadness showed on his face. He then handed Philipse his own share of meat that he had been eating, then sat there quietly with his arms folded.

Lone Wolf continued eating. After a few moments he cut off another large piece of meat and handed it to his brother. "Thank you, Lone Wolf," Rising Bear said as his eyes lit up. "Thank you for all your kindness."

The three ate in silence.

Before they had finished eating, Philipse got up from the fire.

"Rising Bear, I've got something for you. I'll be back in a minute." He left the cave and the two brothers sitting there by themselves.

"How is it that this white knows how to speak our tongue so well?" Lone Wolf asked.

"I taught him myself, Lone Wolf. He is quick to learn. We have had much time to spend together in this cave, seldom venturing out for fear of being seen. He does not know all our words, but he knows many."

Young Philipse returned, bringing with him a small basket.

"Here, Rising Bear, these are all for you."

"Mulberries, my favorite," Rising Bear said. "Are these from your uncle's farm?"

"Yes, Rising Bear," Philipse said, his hands starting to shake. "I picked them when my uncle was away."

"Thank you," Rising Bear said, with a smile. Philipse smiled in turn.

Lone Wolf sensed the affection between these strangest of friends.

"I put the berries in Wicker's Creek so the cold water would keep them fresh. I meant to bring them earlier," Philipse explained.

"What is this 'Wicker's Creek' he speaks of?" Lone Wolf asked.

"That is what the white man calls the Wysquaqua — Wicker's Creek," Rising Bear answered.

The two brothers laughed aloud at the strange-sounding name.

Philipse, with Rising Bear nodding his approval, handed the mulberries over to Lone Wolf.

"No!" Lone Wolf said, pushing them away. "I take nothing from the white man! Nothing!"

***

The following morning Rising Bear once again prepared his special medicine from yellow starflowers, drinking it as soon as it had been made.

"Do you feel better?" Lone Wolf asked, watching with concern.

"Yes, Lone Wolf, somewhat. But I fear my health is failing rapidly. Each time I need more of this medicine for it to work its special cure. My remaining days are few, as you can see from this decrepit body that barely has strength left to make it to the woods to relieve itself."

"Nonsense, Brother. Your medicines and the special powers they wield are strong as ever, as are you. You shall live to see many snows before your days are done."

"I wish it were so, Lone Wolf," Rising Bear answered. "But now there is no doubt. Just this past night I saw an omen in my dreams."

"What omen?" Lone Wolf asked anxiously.

"I saw myself seated alone on the rocks along the shore of the Mahikanittuc," Rising Bear went on to explain in a somber voice. "Then suddenly a huge bird, an eagle with outspread wings, swooped down from behind, snatched me up in its hooked talons, carrying me ever higher into the clouds until I faded out of sight."

There was no question as to the meaning of this dream, Lone Wolf thought. He had no words to calm his brother's just fears.

"While I still have my wits," Rising Bear said, "I must ask you one last favor."

"Yes, Rising bear," Lone Wolf said, "whatever you wish."

"I know for certain, now," Rising Bear said, "that my days are few. And so I ask that when I die, Lone Wolf, you bury me at the foot of the sacred cliffs, in the old way. Then my soul, I pray, may pass over to the Spirit Land, and rest for all time with the people of the past, and with the Great Spirit."

"Fear not, Rising Bear," Lone Wolf assured him. "I hope your remaining days are many. But when your time comes and your spirit is called away, I promise you shall be buried in the old way, on the far shore of the Mahikanittuc, at the foot of the sacred cliffs where the Great Spirit dwells."

"Thank you, Lone Wolf," Rising Bear said with a deep sense of relief. "My soul is now at peace. I will be forever grateful."

***

It was a crisp, sunny day in early fall. The leaves had begun to change color. Lone Wolf was returning from Wysquaqua Creek, where he had taken his morning bath. As he entered the cave and made his way toward the back, he was surprised to find young Philipse there. Philipse was kneeling over Rising Bear who was lying on his bed furs. He was giving him starflower medicine to drink.

"What happened?" Lone Wolf shouted as he neared the two. Philipse stuttered when he began to speak.

"Rising—Rising—Bear is very sick. I gave him all the medicine, but it doesn't seem to work any more."

Lone Wolf knelt down, pushing Philipse out of the way.

"He is only trying to help," Rising Bear said.

Lone Wolf stared into Rising Bear's face. The gentle glows of the fire seemed, for a moment, to restore the radiance of his brother's lost youth.

"Rising Bear, can I bring you something? Medicine? Water?" "There is nothing more, Lone Wolf, that you or anyone can do," Rising Bear answered, his voice weakening at every word. "The sacred drums of the Great Spirit are calling me. I pray that my soul may soon cross the Mahikanittuc, over to the Spirit Land. My heart yearns to see our mother and father again, and the rest

171

of our people. There we shall all be together, as the proud tribe we once were."

"I remember my promise to you, Rising Bear," Lone Wolf reassured him. "You shall be buried in the old way, at the foot of the sacred cliffs."

"Thank you, Lone Wolf. Thank you for having returned to our land and for having dispelled the loneliness which I have lived with for so long."

Rising Bear drew his last breath.

Lone Wolf noticed tears in Philipse's eyes. A tear now flowed down his own face. How strange life was, Lone Wolf thought, that he should be sharing the sorrow for the loss of his brother with a white man, one of those people for whom he carried the deepest hatred.

All was quiet as Lone Wolf held his brother's body in his arms. He looked into the eyes of the brother who had given him the peace of heart that had eluded him all his life, the brother who had revealed the secret his father had taken with him to his grave long ago, the brother who had waited faithfully for Lone Wolf's return.

"Farewell, Rising Bear," Lone Wolf said. "Farewell brother-of-the-same-birth. Forgive me, once again, for the ill-feelings I held against you. I wish I had truly known you."

Lone Wolf closed the eyelids of his brother.

***

The burial preparations, following tribal tradition, kept Lone Wolf busy for much of the day.

Young Philipse returned unexpectedly later that afternoon. "I would've come sooner, Lone Wolf," Philipse explained, "but I had to finish the chores my uncle piled on me." His hands shook once more at the mention of his uncle.

Philipse began immediately to assist Lone Wolf, without any words exchanged between the two. Perhaps Rising Bear had been right after all, Lone Wolf thought for a moment. The boy was a true and loyal friend, unlike the rest of his people. But then, again, he was one of them.

Rising Bear's body had already been wrapped in a burial robe, a thick bear fur. It had served as his blanket, having kept him warm throughout the many winters he spent alone in the cave.

Lone Wolf struggled to carry Rising Bear's body along the narrow ridge just outside the cave. He slipped, then grasped the body at the last moment before it went over the edge. Philipse rushed over to help.

The two then carried the body down the slope to the bank of the river. They placed it in the birch bark canoe readied earlier that day. Inside the canoe was stored the headdresses worn during a burial ritual. Rising Bear had kept these hidden in the cave, along with other artifacts of the tribe.

Lone Wolf pulled out the headdresses, placing one over his head and the other over Philipse's. An astonished look now covered Philipse's face as he stared at Lone Wolf:

The Wolf Clan burial headdress was made from the entire skin of a wolf, including its head. Lone Wolf wore the head of the wolf on top of his own, the mouth of the animal opened wide with its sharp, deadly teeth exposed. Its gray fur was draped over his shoulders and back, like a cape.

Lone Wolf explained to Philipse. "It was the wolf who first led our tribe into this valley long ago, during the time of the great ice. It was the wolf who, throughout the ages, has been the guardian spirit of our People. And in the end, the wolf would escort one's soul as it makes its final journey to the Spirit Land."

Lone Wolf sat at the head of the canoe. He directed Philipse to the rear, with Rising Bear's body lying between.

"The sun is about to set," Lone Wolf said. "There is no time to waste."

They paddled quickly toward the middle of the river, with Lone Wolf on alert for any sudden change in tides. He knew only too well the fury of which the Mahikanittuc was capable. But the Great Spirit was with them this day, as the dark, calm water resembled a lake rather than a flowing river.

They continued to paddle. When only a short distance from the western shore, Lone Wolf stopped the canoe, then held it steady in the water.

"Why are we stopped here?" Philipse asked.

"The burial ritual requires a special prayer, before we land our canoe at the foot of the sacred cliffs."

Lone Wolf stood up near the front of the canoe. With arms outstretched toward the towering cliffs immediately ahead, he prayed aloud:

"Oh, Great Spirit, who dwells amid these ancient cliffs, we humbly ask to set foot upon your sacred soil. We return to You, your faithful son, Rising Bear, a Weckquasgeek of the eastern shore. May You deem him worthy to be counted among your warriors of the eternal sun. And may his spirit rest here for all time with You, Father of all spirits."

The prayer completed, they resumed rowing until reaching the narrow shore. Lone Wolf and Philipse pulled the front of the canoe onto the sand. They carried Rising Bear's body toward the base of the cliffs that towered overhead. With stone implements that had been brought with them, they immedIately dug a grave.

Lone Wolf unwrapped long strips of bark taken from the sacred cedar, then lined the bottom of the grave.

The sun began to set rapidly. Lone Wolf looked up. The sky above the cliffs was aflame in crimson and gold.

"Hurry, Philipse," Lone Wolf said as he looked up again. "We must place Rising Bear into his grave at the very moment the sun touches the top of the cliffs."

Philipse quickly grabbed Rising Bear's feet while Lone Wolf held his shoulders. They placed the outstretched body alongside the open grave and waited.

When the sun appeared to touch the top of the cliffs, Rising Bear was lowered into the bark-lined grave. They quickly covered his body with sandy fill that had been piled to one side, completing the burial just as the sun disappeared below the cliffs.

Lone Wolf prayed aloud, "The Great Spirit has lain down in his stone lodge to rest, and Rising Bear with Him." He concluded his prayers with an ancient chant that had been used by his people for countless burials since the long ago.

As he walked back to the canoe with Philipse, Lone Wolf, using a cedar branch, carefully swept away their footprints behind them. "We must leave no trace of human presence on the sacred soil."

A veil of darkness now settled over the shore, moving slowly from the base of the cliffs, over the fresh grave, then towards the water. Soon the river was covered in darkness.

Lone Wolf struck a flint and lit two torches he had brought with him. He placed them upright into supports on each side of the bow of the canoe.

They pushed the canoe out into the water until free of the sandy bottom, then headed back across the river. As they paddled through the dark, Lone Wolf recounted to Philipse how, in times past, there would have been a long procession of torch-lit canoes crossing the river. But only those warriors escorting the body within the burial canoe were permitted to set foot upon the sacred soil of the Spirit Land, each wearing the Wolf Clan headdress. The others would wait offshore in their canoes, watching from a distance. In one of these canoes, a chosen warrior would beat the sacred drums during each crossing.

When they reached the eastern shore, Lone Wolf dragged the canoe out of the water. He doused the torches in the river. Within thick bushes that grew along the shore, he carefully hid the canoe, together with the torches.

"I have to get back home," Philipse said, "before my uncle comes looking for me."

Lone Wolf noticed the boy's hands shaking again at the mention of his uncle.

Philipse quickly climbed back up the slope, then disappeared into the woods.

Lone Wolf looked over to the distant shore and the ancient cliffs, now shrouded in darkness. He began to worry. When his own time finally comes, who would bury him in the old way, following the Wolf Clan ritual? He was now the last of his kind. There was no one left who knew what needed to be done, nor the special prayers to be recited. No one except Philipse.

For the moment, he felt content that he had kept his promise to his brother. Rising Bear had crossed over to the Spirit Land to rest among those of his tribe buried there long before. He now belonged to the people of the past—and to the Great Spirit.

Rising Bear would never again be alone.

Chapter 18

Vengeance

Many days had passed since Lone Wolf last saw Philipse. Now that Rising Bear was gone, he wondered if the youth would ever return to the cave. He recalled the last time he had seen him, and his hands shaking at the mention of his uncle. Why did Philipse fear him so?

Lone Wolf looked around the cave. It had become his refuge, he realized. He had taken on his brother's reclusive life.

But he could not live this way! He had been the Warrior Chief of a proud people, free to roam the Northern Plains. Now he had become a captive of the white man, cautious to venture out from the secluded cave for fear of being seen.

He must return, then, to the Blackfoot and to his old friend, Bird Rattler. There he could live out his remaining days among the mountains and plains, far from the white man. And he knew that when it was time to pass from this life, the Blackfoot would bury him on Going-to-the-Sun Mountain, alongside his son, Swift Elk.

If he were to remain here in the Eastern Woodlands, then who would bury him? Rising Bear and the Weckquasgeek were all gone. His body would rot away in some remote corner of the woods, or be devoured by animals. Without a burial rite, how could his soul cross over to the Spirit Land? Only a warrior killed in battle, like his own father, could pass directly to the Spirit Land.

He must hunt, then, to secure a supply of meat for his journey back to the Northern Plains. And he must build up his strength, for the difficulties he would again encounter along the way.

After scouting the surrounding woods, Lone Wolf found a patch of blackberry bushes. The juicy berries were a favorite food of wild turkeys, and it was there that they would most likely be feeding at this time of day. It had been a long while since he last tasted turkey. Careful not to scare away his prey, Lone Wolf stood quietly for a moment. He listened for the distinctive gobbling of a tom turkey. Instead, he heard footsteps from behind. He was being followed!

Crouching beneath the brush, he waited for the pursuer to approach. There was a rustle as someone forced his way through the blackberry bushes. Lone Wolf leaped out of his hiding place then grabbed the intruder from behind, wrapping both arms around his neck.

"Lone Wolf, it's me!" came a choking cry. "It's me, Philipse." Lone Wolf released his grip.

Philipse quickly stepped back. There was fear on his face, as he remembered his first encounter with Lone Wolf.

"What are you doing so deep in the forest?" Lone Wolf asked, recalling that the youth seldom ventured far from his uncle's farm.

"I'm hunting," Philipse answered nervously. "I'm trying to track down a deer, like that large buck you brought back to the cave a while ago."

"Why have you taken to the hunt?" Lone Wolf asked. "I thought you raised animals to eat, on your uncle's farm."

"Yes, Lone Wolf. I wanted to visit you at the cave, but felt I should bring a deer to pay you back for all the food you shared with me in the past."

"Is that why you have not returned?"

"Yes, I wanted to bring you the biggest deer you've ever seen, to repay you."

How strange, Lone Wolf thought. The ways of the white man continued to puzzle him.

"There is no need to repay one another," Lone Wolf said. "That is not our way. The Indian shares all that is his. To do otherwise would offend the Great Spirit from whose bounty all gifts come. You are free to visit whenever you wish."

Philipse smiled.

"I will teach you the ways of a hunter," Lone Wolf said, "if you are still intent on taking your own deer." He had not forgotten the kindness the youth had shown towards his brother.

"Yes, please," Philipse said. "But there's one thing, Lone Wolf. Would you mind if I kept the rack of antlers for myself?"

"Do you have need of them to make tools, like our people, for scrapers, or awls, or handles for knives?"

"No, nothing like that. I want to hang them on a wall in my room, for everyone to see."

Indeed, how strange were the ways of the white man, Lone Wolf thought, to make such foolish use of the antlers of a deer.

"Before you can ever take your antlers," Lone Wolf said, "you must first take the deer upon whose head they grow. Doing this requires great skill."

Philipse moved closer to Lone Wolf.

"You would never have gotten a deer with all the noise you made moving through the bushes. A deer would have heard you from far off. The hunter makes no sound as he stalks his prey, no sound at all. You must become a part of the forest, otherwise the deer will know you are there long before you come within sight."

Philipse listened intently as Lone Wolf explained the age-old skills required for hunting.

"Remember, the deer relies on all of its keen senses, any one of which will betray your presence. You must not show yourself, nor make the slightest sound, nor allow the wind to carry your scent back to your prey. So let us now return to the hunt."

Philipse followed Lone Wolf into a remote section of the forest. From a secret cache hidden in the bushes, Lone Wolf removed a spear he had made.

"Here, Phlipse, this is for you, to use on the hunt."

"Thank you!" Philipse said. "It's just like yours."

For the remainder of the morning, Lone Wolf taught Philipse how to use the spear in felling large game. As he showed him the proper way to throw a spear, he put his hand on Philipse's shoulder for a moment. Philipse looked at Lone Wolf and smiled. Lone Wolf smiled, in turn, then caught himself.

"Now it is time for you to prove yourself!" Lone Wolf said to his young student.

Anxious to put into practice all that Lone Wolf had taught him, Philipse made his way deeper into the woods, his mentor right behind him. After hiding in thick shrubs along a brook, Philipse spotted the head of a deer peering from behind a tree on the opposite bank.

The moment the deer came out into the open to drink, Philipse sprang from his hiding place. He drew back the spear Lone Wolf had given him, then threw it at the startled animal. The sharp point found its mark in the lower neck, as Lone Wolf had taught. The deer took two steps and suddenly collapsed to the ground.

Philipse ran toward his prey, leaping over the brook. Lone Wolf followed.

"Lone Wolf, a buck! I got a buck! And look at the size of its antlers!"

"You have done well, Philipse," Lone Wolf said. "Very well, indeed, for such a young hunter. Now we must release its spirit." He knelt down and held the deer's head.

With quick slashes of his knife, Lone Wolf cut off the head of the deer. Philipse watched in horror as the head fell to the ground. Lone Wolf prayed aloud to the deer. "We ask your forgiveness, beloved creature of the forest, and offer thanks for giving up your life so that we may have food." He then positioned the head to face west.

"In this way," Lone Wolf explained to Philipse, "the spirit of the animal will be released from its body the moment the rays of the setting sun illuminate its eyes. It then can cross over to the Spirit Land. One must follow this ritual, lest the spirit of the animal remain forever captive, here in its earthly life. If such were to happen, its spirit would stalk the forests, warning all its kind of the approach of the hunter who so aggrieved it. One would thus always encounter failure on the hunt."

Lone Wolf went on to explain that the following day they could return to remove the antlers. He then helped lift the large buck onto Philipse's shoulders. "A hunter carries his own kill," he said.

"I'll bring him back to the cave by myself," Philipse said proudly. He staggered the first few steps from the heavy load.

As they returned through the forest, Lone Wolf spotted a wild turkey near the patch of blackberries he had seen earlier that day. Without hesitating, Lone Wolf let loose his spear. He would taste turkey once again.

The two reached the hidden cave, carrying their bounty of deer and turkey. There would be roasted meat, enough to last a long while for the two to share.

***

A number of days passed before Philipse returned to the cave that had now become Lone Wolf's refuge. That evening, after the two had finished eating deer meat from Philipse's kill, Lone Wolf unwrapped a fur lying alongside the fire.

"Here, Philipse, these are the antlers from the buck you felled. I returned the following day to remove them, before some scavenger dragged them off." A look of bemusement covered Lone Wolf's face. "For you to hang on your wall. "

181

"Oh thanks, Lone Wolf, for remembering. I would have gotten them myself, but my uncle loaded me down with extra farm chores. Wow, these are the largest antlers I've ever seen!" For a moment, Philipse held the rack high above his head.

"Here, Lone Wolf, I want you to keep them."

"But Philipse, I know how much you had wanted them for yourself."

"No, please. You keep them, for teaching me how to hunt, and for all your kindness."

"You are a thoughtful person," Lone Wolf said. "What might I give you?"

"One of your stories, Lone Wolf, please, a story of these strange-looking animals." Philipse pointed to the wall of the cave, and to an ancient petroglyph of a woolly mammoth.

Lone Wolf, as his own father once recounted to him, told of the time the Weckquasgeek first entered the valley of the Mahikanittuc in the long ago. "Nomadic hunters in search of prey, our ancestors followed the wolves, which they always kept with them, into this land. Here they found a strange animal they had never seen before, the woolly mammoth, whose great size filled them with terror. Over time these creatures were to provide our people with the meat and furs needed to survive the harsh winters during the time of the great ice. As the winters became less severe and new forests covered the land, the mammoths disappeared with the receding glaciers. But our people, the Weckquasgeek, were to remain, growing in number and strength, until the winds of change brought the white man to our shores."

Lone Wolf recounted this and other stories during those evenings when Philipse visited the cave. As Philipse listened to his stories, he came to know Lone Wolf and the tribe to which he and Rising Bear had once belonged. He came to understand all that Lone Wolf and his people had suffered at the hands of the white man, including the loss of their lands and their way of life. And he understood the reasons for the hatred Lone Wolf still carried for the white man, all except Philipse.

After time, a deep trust grew between the two, and they became friends. To Philipse, Lone Wolf had become the father he had never known. And for Lone Wolf, Philipse had become a second son to whom he could teach the skills of a hunter, for his own son, Swift Elk, had long since passed over to the Spirit Land. And at times of doubt, Rising Bear's words would return to mind once again — "one cannot blame the son for the sins of his father."

***

It was an overcast day in autumn. Philipse had been able to break away from the farm to join Lone Wolf in a late afternoon hunt. Again, they scouted the surrounding forest for signs of prey. With cold weather approaching, Lone Wolf had been stocking the cave with a supply of meat to carry him through the winter months, and to prepare for his journey back to the Blackfoot in early spring.

As the two made their way out of the woods into a clearing, they stopped in their tracks. Just ahead was the figure of a man, standing there as though he had been waiting a while. The strained suspenders around his protruding belly appeared ready to snap.

"So that's it! I knew you been up to something," the heavyset figure called out.

"Lone Wolf, it's my Uncle Jacobs," Philipse said, his voice trembling.

"Well, well, so this is why you got no time to do extra chores for me on the farm," Jacobs said. He slowly approached the two. "Got yourself an Injun friend, I see. I figured you was out playing with the other kids or somethin', but never this."

Jacobs looked Lone Wolf over closely. "Well I'll be. I thought you Injuns been long since gone from these parts. I've heard stories of some of your kind being spotted in the forest from time to time, but I didn't believe them."

Jacobs turned to Philipse again. "What you gotta say for yourself, boy?"

"Uncle, I did all my chores for today," Philipse answered, his hands shaking. "I finished early."

"Don't give me no backtalk. You know there's always work to be done around the farm. And what are you doing out here with an Injun, who's trespassing? He's got no right being on my land!"

"But he's my friend, Uncle."

"Friend? I don't want to hear that nonsense. You're not to have anything to do with him or any of his kind. These Injuns are all savages. They can't be trusted. I don't want you to see him anymore!"

"And as for you," Jacobs warned Lone Wolf, "I want you off my land. I want you off now."

"This is really his land," Philipse interrupted as he placed himself between Lone Wolf and his uncle. "All this land once belonged to his people. They were here a long time ago. He told me the story of how they had first come...."

Before Philipse could finish, his uncle slapped him across the face with the back of his hand, knocking him to the ground. The youth's mouth began to bleed.

Lone Wolf watched in shock. Throughout his life he had never seen a grown man strike a boy.

"Don't you ever say that again, that this is his land," Jacobs warned. There was a wild rage in his eyes. "This land is mine, and mine alone! And don't ever take sides with that Injun against me again!"

Philipse picked himself up off the ground.

"Did you forget who takes care of you?" Jacobs said.

"Take care of me?" Philipse answered. "I've been working hard for you ever since I came to the farm."

Jacobs drew back his hand, ready to strike Philipse again.

Lone Wolf jumped between the two.

"Get out of my way, savage, or you'll be next," Jacobs threatened.

Lone Wolf stood firm.

Jacobs put his hands on Lone Wolf, trying to push him out of the way to get at his nephew.

No sooner had Jacobs's hands touched his chest than Lone Wolf knocked him to the ground. Jacobs lay stretched out on his back, his face hidden behind his protruding belly.

After regaining his senses, Jacobs struggled to get to his feet. He stared at the two of them, standing side by side. His face turned red.

"If I had my musket with me, savage, I'd finish you off now. I'm warning you one last time, get off and stay off my land! If I catch you here again, I'll shoot you on sight!"

Dusting himself off, Jacobs began to walk away. He turned around. "I mean it! I want you off my land or you're as good as dead!"

Jacobs disappeared into the woods.

Hatred flared in Lone Wolf's heart. If Jacobs ever returned, Lone Wolf promised himself, he would be the one to be killed. The man did not deserve to live.

Lone Wolf and Philipse headed back to the cave, watchful that they were not being followed. Along the way Lone Wolf stripped bark from a willow tree and applied the juice from the soft, inner layer to Philipse's swollen lip.

They entered the cave and remained there a while, sitting in silence. There was a sadness on Philipse's face that Lone Wolf had never seen before.

"I'm afraid, Lone Wolf," Philipse broke the silence. "I'm afraid for you. My uncle is vengeful. I don't want him to hurt you."

"Do not fear for me, good friend," Lone Wolf answered. "I have known his type before. Each that dared to confront me, I made short work of."

"Do what you have to do, Lone Wolf, to defend yourself."

"My spear point is sharp and at the ready for your uncle's return, should he be so foolish. Never again shall the white man drive me from my land!"

Lone Wolf gently placed his hand on Philipse's shoulder. "And should your uncle harm you, he will live to regret it."

"I have to leave now," Philipse said, his hands shaking again. He left the cave to return to the farm.

As he watched the figure of his friend disappear through the opening, Lone Wolf felt sorrow for him, a feeling he never had before for any white man.

How cruel it was, Lone Wolf thought, for a grown man to strike a boy. No Indian would ever dishonor himself by such a savage act. The Weckquasgeek treated children, and women, gently and kindly. This had always been their way, the old way.

That night Lone Wolf had trouble falling asleep. He kept brooding over Jacobs' warning, "Get off and stay off my land!" He was being driven out, again, from his ancestral lands. Images now flashed through Lone Wolf's mind: his village in flames; survivors being rounded up for the forced march; the charred bodies of his people thrown into a pit.

Again hatred flared in his heart, a seething hatred for Jacobs and all his kind.

Lone Wolf now also feared for Philipse. His uncle had struck him viciously. No one would be there to protect his young friend, once Lone Wolf left to return to the Blackfoot.

He must kill Jacobs! He must kill him before he left, for Philipse's sake, and to avenge the sufferings of his people.

For Jacobs was everything he hated in the white man.

Chapter 19

Last of the Weckquasgeek

Stillness settled over the forest and over Lone Wolf's spirit. The animals were now few, most having gone into their winter dens. Each evening Lone Wolf waited for Philipse to return to the cave. But he had not come back since the encounter with his uncle.

As Lone Wolf wandered alone through the darkening woods, he passed a log cabin at the edge of a clearing. From a distance he gazed a while into a window illuminated in glowing light. There, inside, was a family of white settlers gathered around the fireplace: mother, father and two children. How Lone Wolf now yearned to return to that earlier time of his life, when only the Weckquasgeek inhabited these ancient forests and his own family lived here together. But they were all gone. He had become an outcast in his native land.

His brother's words came back to haunt him. "There is a loneliness in this life that one can never know, unless he has lived it."

This would pass, Lone Wolf reminded himself. He would return to the Blackfoot in early spring, after the Spirit of the Snows had retreated to his den.

It was night when Lone Wolf got back to the cave. There, near the campfire, was a basket of mulberries. Philipse had been there. He must seek him out!

Early the following morning Lone Wolf made his way through the forest to Jacobs' farm. Hiding within thick brush at the edge of a wooded hill, he looked below to where Philipse and his uncle were at work.

"Why are you resting?" Jacobs yelled out. "You better finish chopping those logs or you'll get no breakfast."

Philipse, standing next to a pile of wood, strained to pull the axe head out of a log after it had become wedged.

"I'm going in for my breakfast," Jacobs said. "You stay out here until you finish all your work."

Lone Wolf, watching Philipse standing there alone, felt pity for him. So this is why the youth was unable to visit the cave.

Philipse was a captive, Lone Wolf thought, a captive of Jacobs, trapped on his farm. But then so was he, a captive of Jacobs, trapped in the cave, forbidden to set foot onto his own ancestral lands!

Lone Wolf's hatred turned to rage.

"I must kill him," Lone Wolf said to himself. "I must kill this demon once and for all, to free us both from his evil!"

He returned to the cave.

In his dreams that night, Lone Wolf saw himself standing again on the ridge-of-the-three-pines, overlooking the Mahikanittuc. Facing the cliffs on the far shore, he had returned to seek out the Great Spirit. At the very moment a vision was to appear, he awoke.

The sun was beginning to rise when Lone Wolf anxiously made his way to the ridge. For all that day, Lone Wolf remained on the edge of the overlook, without food or water. He prayed in silence. As the sun moved into the western sky, he finally called out to the distant cliffs:

"Why, Great Spirit, have you summoned me in my dreams, to return here once more?"

There was silence.

"Speak to me, Great Spirit, You who have eluded me all of my life."

Again, there was no answer, only the wind as it blew across the river from the distant cliffs.

Lone Wolf was overcome by a strange sense of detachment from the world that surrounded him. He felt he was all alone, as though the Great Spirit had created him at the center of this world of mortals, the Great Spirit who was forever testing him. All those around him, his family, his people, even the hated white man, had been placed here on earth for the purpose of putting his soul to the test throughout its life-long journey. And now in his old age, the Great Spirit had not yet finished with him.

Later that day he began to feel faint from the lack of water. As the sun moved lower in the western sky, a vision finally appeared:

Rays of crimson and gold reflected off the waters below, creating a glittering pathway of light across the river. From the base of the towering cliffs on the far shore, a lone rider galloped across the sandy bank. Lone Wolf watched as the horse and rider, without breaking stride, leaped onto the water, then followed the gleaming pathway of light.

He could not believe his eyes. The horse galloped on the surface of the water, carrying its rider safely across the river.

Within moments, the specter reached the rocky shore immediately below the ridge. Its powerful mount, again without breaking stride, climbed the steep slope and headed toward Lone Wolf.

The specter dismounted, then turned to face him.

"Father, you have finally come!"

"Yes, Lone Wolf."

They stepped to within arm's reach of each other.

"It is good to see you, Father, and to speak to you at long last. But I beg, do not flee again!"

"No, Lone Wolf, I will not flee. I heard you cry out to the Great Spirit. He has allowed me to journey back, once again, across the river that separates our two worlds. I am here to share with you a matter of the greatest importance."

"I know, Father. Before he died, Rising Bear revealed to me what had long lain buried in your heart—

that you deemed me worthy to succeed you as Warrior Chief of our people."

"Yes, Lone Wolf. Rising Bear, after crossing over to the Spirit Land, told me that he had already spoken to you. But there is another matter, more important, that I must share with you."

"What can be more important, Father, than to wear the prized headdress of a Warrior Chief?"

"Your soul, Lone Wolf, your immortal soul."

"I do not understand."

"I come to warn you, before it is too late!"

"Warn me? Warn me of what, Father?"

"Your soul is in great peril!"

"How can this be? I have always prayed to the Great Spirit."

"Do you remember, Lone Wolf, when you last chased me through the forest, and I led you to the Spirit of The Word, suspended in the tree? And do you remember what he had said to you?"

"To seek out and make peace with my brother. But I have done that, Father. Rising Bear and I became friends, before he died."

"Yes, I felt great joy and relief that my sons had finally reconciled, since I unwittingly had been the cause of your ill feelings by having put you at odds with one another. But there is another matter of equal importance."

Lone Wolf did not answer. There was a worried look on his face.

"The Spirit of The Word told you that you must also forgive the white man, as He forgave those who hung Him in the tree of torment. You cannot ignore his words, Lone Wolf, for they are of the Great Spirit. The hatred you still carry for the white man, and for this Jacobs, has corrupted your soul."

"Father, lest we forget! The white man has committed great evil against the Weckquasgeek! He has killed our people — you, long before your time; he has taken our land; and destroyed our way of life. And this Jacobs is the worst of all, one who strikes a young boy. My hatred is well justified."

"When you stand before the Great Spirit, Lone Wolf, and your soul is seething with hatred for one He calls his own, one whose sufferings you do not know, how then can He deem you worthy to enter the Spirit Land?"

"Why, Father, even now from out of your grave, do you put me to the test? Have I not proven myself, time and again throughout my life?"

"It is not I, Lone Wolf, it is the Great Spirit who puts you to the test, as He does to all men. If you strike down this Jacobs out of hatred, you are no longer worthy to be called a warrior. You will become like him whom you despise."

"My hatred runs deep. It has been carried over a lifetime. It is too late for me to change," Lone Wolf pleaded.

"It is never too late," his father said. "You must purge from your soul the hatred you carry for this man and those of his race. Otherwise their evil will possess your spirit, holding it forever captive."

Lone Wolf stood there quietly, looking into the face of the father he had always tried to please.

"I believe in you, Lone Wolf, and in your goodness. Pray to the Great Spirit, that He may give you the courage to change. And above all, listen to your conscience. For it is the conscience, silent voice of the soul, to which one must always answer."

"I will try, Father," Lone Wolf said.

"My time is nearly gone," his father said anxiously as he glanced up at the position of the sun. "But remember this, Lone Wolf, and remember it well. You will never look upon the face of the Great Spirit if your heart remains corrupted with hatred. And when your spirit crosses the Mahikanittuc on its final journey, neither will it be allowed to enter the Spirit Land, and to join there the people of the past. It will remain lost in this world, forever adrift on the river, floating endlessly with the ever-changing tide."

Fear came over Lone Wolf's face. The vision he had sought throughout his life carried with it the gravest of warnings, putting him to the test as never before.

His father embraced Lone Wolf. Again glancing up at the sun, he pulled himself away, then quickly mounted up. Before riding off he addressed Lone Wolf with a reassuring voice. "Farewell, great Warrior Chief. You have long since proven yourself to me. Now you must prove yourself, one last time, to the Great Spirit whose drums will soon call you home."

Turning his horse around abruptly, Lone Wolf's father drove the mount down the slope and, without breaking stride, leaped onto the surface of the water below. As they galloped across the river, the glittering pathway of light began to disappear immediately behind them. The moment they reached the far shore, the rays of the setting sun faded beneath the cliffs, casting all in darkness.

Lone Wolf fell into a deep sleep, there on the ridge-of-the-three-pines that overlooked the Mahikanittuc. In his dreams he saw his own spirit, forever adrift on the river, floating endlessly with the ever-changing tide.

***

The rays of the rising sun crept over Lone Wolf's face, waking him out of his sleep.

His thoughts returned to the vision of the previous day, and to his father's warning. Throughout his life, Lone Wolf's courage had never failed him. It had sustained him in all battles, against all enemies, mortal and spirit alike. But how could he overcome his hatred of the white man that ran so deep?

Was he not justified in this hatred of those who had caused so much suffering: the white settlers who had taken his tribal lands; the Dutch militia that burned the village, killing his people, and his father; Sergeant Cody and the death of his mother during the forced march; the white fur trader whose coughing sickness took his wife; and now Jacobs?

His was a hatred that had seethed like a smoldering fire throughout his life. But if he failed this last test, Lone Wolf knew he would never again see his father, nor his people.

Kneeling down as he faced the ancient cliffs, Lone Wolf prayed to the Great Spirit one last time.

Before leaving the ridge, he sharpened the stone point of his spear.

***

Later that morning Philipse made his way through the woods. He looked behind to make sure he was not being followed.

Finding the cave empty, Philipse searched the surrounding forest for Lone Wolf's tracks. He then followed them toward the river.

Lone Wolf was about to leave the ridge when Philipse approached. Pleased to see his young friend again, he motioned for them to sit down on a nearby rock.

"Why has it been such a while since your last visit?" Lone Wolf asked.

"My uncle's been keeping a close watch on me," Philipse answered, "ever since that time he threatened you, Lone Wolf. And he's loaded me down with extra chores. A number of times I tried to visit you at the cave, but he followed me into the woods. I outsmarted him by hiding in the bushes, then doubling back to the farm. This time, though, there shouldn't be any problem. I overheard my uncle say, before he left this morning, he would be away most of the day."

"We have time to visit then," Lone Wolf said.

"But why are you here at the ridge, instead of at the cave?" Philipse asked.

"I came to seek a vision," Lone Wolf said. "But I received a warning instead. I can never enter the Spirit Land as long as my soul is burdened with the hatred I carry for Jacobs."

"I know how you feel, Lone Wolf," Philipse said. "I used to hate my uncle in a way you can't believe. I hated the very sight of him. At times, I wished he was dead, and even thought of ways of killing him. It was making me sick inside, turning me bitter, like him. Then I met Rising Bear."

"Rising Bear!" Lone Wolf said. "What did Rising Bear have to do with this?"

"Well, when I explained to him the way I felt, he taught me to hate in a different way."

"How so?" Lone Wolf asked.

"Rising Bear taught me that it was all right to hate all the cruel things my uncle did. But that I should feel sorrow for my uncle, as well, because of the way he was raised when he was a boy himself."

"What way was that?" Lone Wolf asked Philipse, surprised he had never spoken of this before.

"I overheard my aunt tell a friend that when my uncle was a boy, his own father would beat him. He used a leather strap, she said. And his father, whenever he had one of his fits of rage, would chase him out of the house at night, into the cold."

"That is sad, very sad," Lone Wolf said. "I never thought that someone like Jacobs, who is cruel towards others, was once the victim of such cruelty himself."

"Well, he was, Lone Wolf," Philipse said, "and ever since Rising Bear explained things to me, I understand why my uncle is the way he is. And though I still hate what he does, I can't really hate him anymore the way I once did. I feel sorry for him now. Like Rising Bear said about my uncle, 'His spirit is captive to the abuse he suffered as a child.'"

"How terrible it must be," Lone Wolf said, "never to know the love of one's father. Such an unfair burden for the soul of a young boy to bear."

They sat quietly for a while. The only sound was of the wind as it blew from across the river.

"You are young, but you are wise beyond your years," Lone Wolf said.

"Well, Rising Bear was the one who was wise," Philipse said. "They were his words."

"But you listened, and you took his words to heart."

Lone Wolf placed his hand on Philipse's shoulder. The two friends left to return to the cave.

***

On their way back through the woods, they crossed the open area where Lone Wolf's village had once stood. Suddenly there was the cry of a bird. Lone Wolf looked up to see a white-headed eagle circling above the river. It glided effortlessly on the warm updrafts, then flew toward the sacred cliffs on the far shore.

"An omen!" Lone Wolf said.

"What does it mean?" Philipse asked.

Lone Wolf did not answer.

They continued on their way across the clearing. From out of the woods, a short distance ahead, Jacobs suddenly appeared. He was carrying a musket.

"I thought I'd catch you two out here again," he shouted from across the way. "Figured I was going out for the day, did you, Nephew? But I tricked you this time and hid in the woods, waiting for you to lead me to him."

Lone Wolf held his spear at the ready. He stepped in front of Philipse, shielding him from his uncle.

"I warned you, savage, didn't I?" Jacobs yelled. "I warned you to get off my land, but you didn't listen!"

Jacobs raised the musket to his shoulder, then aimed the long barrel. The flint strike jammed.

"Quick, Lone Wolf, throw your spear before he gets another chance to shoot."

Lone Wolf did not answer.

"Quick, Lone Wolf, quick!" Philipse shouted again. "Throw it, now! You have to defend yourself."

Lone Wolf raised his spear.

Jacobs continued to have trouble with the jammed flint strike.

Lone Wolf turned toward the river, and gazed a moment at the distant cliffs. He suddenly threw his spear into the ground, the stone point disappearing beneath the surface.

"No! No!" Philipse cried out.

"A true warrior does not throw his spear in hatred," Lone Wolf said in a calm voice.

The crack of a musket shot echoed off the surrounding trees. A cloud of smoke enveloped Jacobs.

The musket ball struck Lone Wolf in the chest. He fell to the ground.

"Lone Wolf!" Philipse cried out. He knelt down beside him, and held his head in his arms. "Lone Wolf, you should have thrown your spear when you had the chance."

"No, Philipse, I could not. It would have been an act of vengeance. My spirit would then have become captive to the evil of this man and those like him."

Jacobs ran across the clearing, panting heavily. He stood there, looking down at the two figures.

"Why did you do this, Uncle? Why did you have to shoot him? Didn't you see his spear sticking in the ground?"

"Yes, I saw it. But I warned him to stay off my land, didn't I? The law says I got a right to protect my property and keep trespassers off. No matter, he's only a savage!"

Lone Wolf looked up at Jacobs. As he began to speak, blood flowed from the corner of his mouth. "You have taken my land, and my way of life. But not my spirit."

His eyes began to close.

"When he dies," Jacobs said, "don't bury him here on my property. Roll him down to the edge of the river. Then take kerosene from the barn and burn his body. We don't want any trace left of him, or his kind."

Lone Wolf's eyes opened again. He looked up at Jacobs. "One day you, too, must answer to the Great Spirit."

"I don't believe in any of that," Jacobs said. He turned and left.

Lone Wolf's face was peaceful as he lay on the ground, his head in Philipse's arms.

"Why didn't you kill him?" Philipse asked. "You had the right to defend yourself."

"My conscience would not allow it," Lone Wolf answered. "For then I would have killed the young boy who still lives and suffers within him, the boy who never knew the love of his father."

Philipse wiped the dust from Lone Wolf's face. Lone Wolf's breathing began to slow. Blood from his chest wound flowed onto Philipse's pants.

"I'll get you the special medicines Rising Bear made," Philipse said anxiously. "There're still some left in the cave."

"There is no need," Lone Wolf said. "My journey is done. The white-headed eagle waits no longer."

"I'm afraid, Lone Wolf, afraid for you, and for myself."

"Fear not for me," Lone Wolf said. "My spirit is free at last. It is captive to no man, and to no passion."

Philipse held Lone Wolf tightly in his arms, looking down at him. There were the pensive eyes of one

198

who had seen the loss of all those he had loved. And there was the weathered face of an old hunter and warrior whose people were no more. He was the last of his kind, the last of the Weckquasgeek.

Lone Wolf, swallowing his own blood, struggled to speak.

"Fear not for yourself, good friend. Let nothing disturb you, nothing affright you. All things of this world are passing. The Great Spirit alone never changes. Believe in Him, and you will want for nothing."

"I'll always remember your words, Lone Wolf," Philipse said, tears swelling in his eyes. "Can I get you some water?"

"No, Philipse. One last wish...bury..." Lone Wolf's voice grew weaker. "Bury me in the old way, as we did Rising Bear, at the foot of the sacred cliffs."

"I promise, Lone Wolf, I promise I will," Philipse answered. "But I don't want you to die. I love you."

"The Great Spirit took my son," Lone Wolf said. "Then He sent you, to fill the loneliness in my heart."

"The Great Spirit took my father," Philipse answered as tears flowed down his face. "Then He sent you, in his place."

"I hear the call of distant drums," Lone Wolf said.

His eyes slowly closed.

Chapter 20

Distant Drums

An eagle soars above the river, silhouetted against the distant cliffs. Its keen eyes search the eastern shore, but the forests below are now empty.

***

Entering the deserted cave, Philipse walked to where the campfire had once burned. There, alongside the blackened stones, he retrieved the bear fur which Lone Wolf had used for bedding. It would now serve as his burial robe.

Philipse looked down at the charred wood of the campfire. Over its flames he had shared both food and story with Rising Bear and Lone Wolf. From its glows were illuminated the old, wrinkled faces of the two brothers who had befriended him. But now they were gone, the only ones who ever cared for him.

It was late afternoon. Philipse returned to the wooded area where Lone Wolf's body lay hidden under a pile of leaves. There was no time to waste. He must keep his promise. Philipse removed the leaves, then wrapped the body in the bear fur. He lifted the heavy load over his shoulder and made his way down the slope to the bank of the river. Retrieving the canoe from the bushes where Lone Wolf had hidden it, he dragged it to the edge of the water. After placing the body into the canoe, he jumped in and pushed off the sandy bottom. As he put on the wolf-head fur, he recalled its meaning: the hunting wolves that had first led his ancestors into this valley in the long ago, would now escort Lone Wolf on his final journey to the Spirit Land.

Paddling out into the river, Philipse noticed the tide had started to flow in. The dark but still calm waters that surrounded his canoe mirrored the distant cliffs with their weathered face.

He rowed past the middle of the river and approached the western shore. A short distance out, he stopped the canoe, then stood with his arms outstretched toward the towering cliffs immediately ahead. Following the burial rite as Lone Wolf had taught him, he recited the special prayer:

"Oh, Great Spirit, who dwells amid these ancient cliffs, I humbly ask to set foot upon your sacred soil. I return to You your faithful son, Lone Wolf, Warrior Chief of the Weckquasgeek — and the last of his kind. May You deem him worthy to be counted among your warriors of the eternal sun. And may his spirit rest here for all time with You, Father of all spirits."

Philipse continued rowing until he reached the western shore. Struggling at first to unload Lone Wolf's body, he carried it inland a short distance toward the base of the cliffs. He looked up, keeping close watch on the sun as it was about to set above the cliffs that towered overhead.

After digging a grave, Phlipse lined it with strips of cedar bark. He waited until the sun appeared to touch the top of the cliffs, then lowered Lone Wolf into the grave. Alongside he laid the spear that the Weckquasgeek had carried on his hunts. The feathered warbonnet of Warrior Chief he carefully placed on Lone Wolf's head. Noticing the small buckskin pouch Lone Wolf always had with him, Philipse opened it. Inside was a tuft of gray hair. He closed it and placed it next to Lone Wolf's heart.

As the sun disappeared behind the cliffs, he covered the body with sandy fill. Darkness began to settle over the narrow shore.

Philipse concluded the prayer of burial, his eyes filled with tears. "The Great Spirit has lain down in his stone lodge to rest, and Lone Wolf with Him."

The moment he returned to the shore, Philipse took a long drink from the river. How foolish, he thought, after finally tasting the salty water carried in by the tide. Already he could feel its effect.

He walked over to the canoe and, lighting two torches, placed them on either side of the bow. After pushing the canoe into deeper water, he began to paddle back across the river. When only a short distance out, he heard drums from the narrow shore below the cliffs. A gentle wind began to blow.

Turning the canoe around, Philipse again faced the cliffs. He strained his eyes as a shape appeared from out of the darkness. There, standing next to the fresh grave, was the figure of a man, his back turned toward the river. The area surrounding the figure was now bathed in twilight, becoming brighter as Philipse watched.

Suddenly, from out of the narrow strip of forest that grew along the base of the cliffs, a riderless horse appeared. The animal galloped over toward the figure at the grave, then neighed. As it came into view, Philipse recognized it from the stories he had heard Lone Wolf tell: the brown and white pinto, Wacanga, Lone Wolf's trusted horse.

The figure mounted up then turned to face the river.

"Lone Wolf!" Philipse shouted across the short expanse of water that separated the two. "Is that you, Lone Wolf?"

Wearing the eagle-feathered headdress of Warrior Chief, and holding his spear upright, Lone Wolf raised his arm in greeting.

Philipse raised his arm, in turn.

Now standing in the canoe, only a short distance from the shore, Philipse watched in disbelief. But how could this be?

Again Philipse heard drums from the narrow strip of forest along the base of the cliffs. Two mounted figures appeared from out of the darkness beneath the trees. They galloped toward Lone Wolf, pulling up in front of him.

From the many stories Lone Wolf had recounted to him, Philipse knew he could recognize the people whom Lone Wolf had cared about in his earthly life. He waited, in anticipation, for the two figures to reveal themselves.

The first rider to greet Lone Wolf was his father, Gray Eagle, wearing a roach headdress with the single feather of a warrior. He pulled up alongside Lone Wolf, to his right. Both now faced the river.

Next, Rising Bear raised his arm in greeting to his brother. Wearing a medicine pouch suspended from his shoulder, he pulled up his horse alongside their father's.

A third time Philipse heard drums from the narrow strip of forest along the base of the cliffs. Again, two riders galloped over to Lone Wolf, pulling up in front of him.

Resplendent in his fur robe of the Great Buffalo, Swift Elk greeted his father. Lone Wolf embraced him. Swift Elk, riding the horse that had been buried with him, pulled up alongside Lone Wolf, to his left.

The last rider to approach wore a buffalo-horned headpiece. Extending to each other their outstretched arms, in the custom of the Blackfoot, Bird Rattler greeted his old friend. He pulled his horse alongside Swift Elk's, so that all five riders were now side by side, facing the river.

It was becoming difficult for Philipse to see. His canoe, still a short distance off shore, was carried farther out into the river with the ever-shifting tide. Down along the shoreline Philipse was able to make out a small village of wigwams. There, too, were figures of men, women and children, going about the village in its peaceful setting along the edge of the water.

Lone Wolf left the others, and galloped down to the village. Out of one of the lodges, two women appeared. He dismounted, then ran over to embrace each of them: first his mother, then his wife, Spring Woman.

At a distance farther down shore, well beyond the village, were herds of deer and buffalo, grazing on the lush grasses that grew everywhere. But how could this be, Philipse wondered. For there, at the outskirts of the grazing herds were giant woolly mammoths, appearing like the images painted on the walls of the cave by Lone Wolf's ancestors.

Philipse could not believe his eyes. Surely the salt water he drank from the river was affecting his mind. But there, a short distance ahead, were both people and animals from the past, going about as they had done during their earthly lives.

How Philipse yearned to return to shore, there to join Lone Wolf. But no matter how hard he paddled, the ever-changing currents kept carrying his canoe farther out into the river.

Again Philipse heard drums. Bright glows of crimson and gold radiated from within the forest at the base of the cliffs. Lone Wolf and the other mounted riders slowly made their way into the woods. A peaceful bliss covered each of their faces.

Lone Wolf was the last to enter the forest. He turned and raised his arm in farewell to Philipse, then disappeared.

"Lone Wolf!" Philipse cried out. "Come back, Lone Wolf! Come back!"

After all had passed from sight, the bright glow from within the forest began to fade.

A veil of darkness now settled over the shore. The drums fell silent.

Philipse again paddled hard, trying to force the canoe back toward the cliffs. But again the shifting currents carried him farther out into the river. Realizing his efforts were futile, he turned the canoe around. With the burning torches facing the eastern shore, he rowed his way back.

All was quiet, except the sound of Philipse's paddle slashing through the water. He would be the last, he thought, to ferry a Weckquasgeek on the sacred crossing of the Mahikanittuc. The ancient burial rite, followed faithfully since the long ago, had now come to an end—like the very people who had believed in it, and in its eternal promise.

Philipse looked back one last time to the cliffs, now shrouded in darkness. He felt a deep solace knowing Lone Wolf's life journey had led him to the Spirit Land. There he would live again amongst his people, free to roam and to hunt as he had done throughout his earthly life.

"Some day, Lone Wolf, when my own life is done, I hope to join you there. But first I, too, have to prove myself."

***

Early the following morning, Philipse awoke. It was dark out. He recalled the words last spoken to him by his Uncle Jacobs just the night before:

"Keep in mind, Nephew, this land one day could all be yours...if you behave yourself."

While his uncle was still asleep, Philipse dressed quickly and left the house. He then took a horse from out of the barn and rode off quietly. A great sense of relief came over him as he left the farm and headed into the forest. He brought with him the spear that Lone Wolf had made for him. Having discarded his own clothing, he was now dressed in buckskin. On his head was the single-feathered head roach once worn by Lone Wolf.

He returned to the secluded ridge-of-the-three-pines. Kneeling on one knee, as he once saw Lone Wolf do, he gazed at the cliffs on the distant shore.

"Lone Wolf! Lone Wolf!" Philipse cried out.

There was no answer.

He called out again to Lone Wolf. His voice became lost in the expanse of water that separated their two worlds.

Philipse waited, then prayed aloud to the Great Spirit. But again there was no answer, only the wind as it blew from across the river.

Philipse recalled Lone Wolf's words, "The Great Spirit speaks to us not in the thunder of a raging storm, but in the whisper of the gentlest wind."

Philipse looked up toward the western sky. The clouds slowly drifted beyond the cliffs, carried by the wind. He realized now what he must do. The time had come to undertake his own journey. He would leave the ancient forests of the Weckquasgeek forever. He would travel west, to the land where native tribes still reigned free. And, like Lone Wolf, he would hunt the buffalo, in their endless herds.

As he was about to leave the ridge, a sudden storm blew down the valley, turning the sky dark. Strong winds began to gust, carrying with them a squall of snow which fell heavily for a moment. Spears of lightning shot from the swiftly-moving clouds, striking the river surface below. Philipse recalled Lone Wolf's stories about his journey back East, and the three spirits of nature he had encountered along the way. It were as though these same spirits of Snow, Fire and Wind had returned to pay their last respects to the Warrior Chief with whom each had done battle.

After mounting up, Philipse made his way through the woods toward the Pocantico, the northern boundary of Lone Wolf's ancestral lands. Just beyond, the Mahikanittuc was narrower and easier to cross. When he reached the Pocantico, he looked back one last time to the woodlands where he had lived since a child, and had shared with Lone Wolf during that final winter. This was the land that Lone Wolf's ancestors had first entered in a time long forgotten, led there by their hunting wolves when the great ice covered much of the earth. And they had remained there ever since, its soil sanctified by their blood.

But the forests were now empty. The drums of the Weckquasgeek had been silenced forever.

And there, on the distant shore, were the ancient cliffs that towered above the river, appearing as they had since the long ago —forever unchanged, like the Great Spirit who had always dwelt there.

Epilogue

"All things of this world are passing"

I. The Blackfoot
Masters of the Northern Plains

The Blackfoot Indians of Northwest Montana and Canada ruled for many years as undisputed masters of the Northern Plains, considered the most powerful and warlike nation north of the Missouri River. They guarded fiercely the mountains and plains they considered sacred, and remained one of only a few Native American tribes never forced from their ancestral lands. They were bitter enemies of American whites for years after their first encounter on July 27, 1806, when two Blackfoot were killed, one shot by Captain Meriwether Lewis of the Lewis and Clark Expedition.

An Algonquin people long separated from the tribes of the Eastern Woodlands, the Blackfoot were made up of three divisions: the Siksika (Blackfoot, from their blackened moccasins), the Kainah ("Blood", from the red-earthen face paint worn during battle), and the Piegan (or Pikuni). Their very existence as nomadic hunters depended upon the buffalo, which was the focal point of their tribal culture, together with veneration of the horse.

With the demise of the great buffalo herds by the 1880's, the proud Blackfoot were no longer able to provide for their own needs, suffering through Starvation Winter of 1883-1884. By treaty, large portions of their lands were ceded to the U.S. Government. Subsequently, remaining tracts near the Marias River were confiscated under executive orders issued by Presidents Ulysses S. Grant and Rutherford B. Hayes, in violation of earlier treaties. The most mountainous region of their ancestral lands, over which they had hunted and roamed freely for generations, has become present-day Glacier National Park.

Descendants of the Blackfoot live today on reservations in Browning, Montana and Alberta, Canada.

II. The Tribes "Resettled"
Loss of Their Lands

The area west of the Mississippi was to become the unwanted destination for various tribes of the Eastern Woodlands and of the Southeast (e.g., Delaware, Cherokee), as they were forcibly removed from their ancestral lands. Following adoption by Congress in 1830 of the Indian Removal Act, the fate of numerous woodland tribes of the East was sealed forever, as President Andrew Jackson pursued its enforcement vigorously — in violation of a Supreme Court ruling declaring the law unconstitutional. The forced removal of the Cherokee to Oklahoma during the winter of 1838 and 1839 resulted in over one quarter of their tribe, men, women, and children, dying along the difficult journey. Once resettled in the new Indian Territory, the haphazard mixing of Indian people hastened the disintegration of individual tribal identity and culture. In the end, entire tribes ceased to exist. Much of their land was incorporated into the new states, which eagerly laid claim to the Indian Territory.

Vast areas of the Great Plains were to become farms, ranches and grazing range. The introduction of barbed wire (1881) facilitated the fencing off of large, privately-owned tracts of land. The huge buffalo herds that had once numbered over 75 million before the white man's arrival,[2] were by 1900 driven to near extinction

---

[2]*Ernest Thompson Seton, a Naturalist (from The Buffalo Book, by David A. Day, Sage Books).*

from indiscriminate slaughter. In 1907 the New York Zoological Society shipped fifteen buffalo from the Bronx Zoo to the Wichita Mountains Wildlife Refuge in Oklahoma to help prevent extinction of the animal that symbolized the freedom of the Great Plains, and which at an earlier time had been able to turn the plains black in its seemingly endless numbers.

With the demise of the huge buffalo herds in the 1880's, the tribal culture and way of life of the Blackfoot were irreversibly changed, as it was for all other nomadic hunters of the plains, and the image of the free-roaming Indian disappeared forever from the American landscape.

Other tribes of the Northern Plains were "resettled" to reservations during the period from the end of the Civil War (1865) to the conclusion of the Indian Wars in December, 1890 (Wounded Knee). Included amongst these were the powerful and warlike Dakota-Sioux, and the Cheyenne, Comanche, Arapaho, Crow, Kutenai and Shoshoni. Tribal ownership of land on such reservations, vital to the preservation of Indian culture and identity, has for years been seriously undermined by ever-changing federal policies including the Land Allotment Act of 1887. The Bureau of Indian Affairs also encouraged individual land sales and mineral leases to outside private interests. Numerous reservations within the Great Plains have long since been broken up, and have passed into private ownership.

With the disappearance of their original tribal lands and hunting grounds, so, too, have disappeared those Native Americans whose very identity was inseparable from the ancestral lands they considered sacred.

III. The Weckquasgeek
People of the Eastern Woodlands

The Weckquasgeek, an Algonquin-speaking people of the Eastern Woodlands, inhabited the eastern shore of the lower Hudson River (c.8,000 B.C.), following the end of the last Ice Age when woolly mammoths still thrived in the emerging forests. Together with surrounding tribes, they called themselves "Mahicans" — People of "the river that flows both ways." They belonged to, and were the most powerful tribe of the Wappinger Confederacy. By the late seventeen hundreds, following the American Revolution, they disappeared from their ancestral lands, their drums silenced forever. No pure-blood Weckquasgeek remains today.

The lands claimed by the Weckquasgeek once ran from what is now the upper half of Manhattan Island, north to the Pocantico River in Sleepy Hollow, New York. Under constant pressure from early Dutch and English settlers (1624, 1664), their wooded hunting grounds were cleared for farms. Amongst these were the large manors of the Van Cortlandt and Philipseburg families. During the late 1800's, the lands facing the Hudson became sprawling, baronial estates of wealthy industrialists, including the properties of Jay Gould and his son Edwin (which encompassed the original campsite of the main Weckquasgeek village known as "Weckquasguck," in present-day Dobbs Ferry, N.Y.). The area has long since been developed for residential and industrial uses, including railroad tracks along the eastern shoreline of the Hudson River (Mahikanittuc).

The ancient cliffs, known as the Hudson Palisades, have been preserved and protected as part of the Palisades Interstate Park —created in 1900 when Theodore Roosevelt, then Governor of New York State, appointed George W. Perkins to head a new commission to safeguard the cliffs on the western shore of the river from quarrying operations that were already underway.

These cliffs appear today much as they did at the end of the last Ice Age when nomadic bands of Paleo-Indians, ancestors of the Weckquasgeek, first entered the Hudson Valley in search of prey. As they watched the sun set above the distant cliffs, the sky aglow in rays of crimson and gold, they believed this was the very place where the Great Spirit dwelt.

Weckquasguck—Mahikanittuc
William Pisani
(Dobbs Ferry, New York)